I0606699

All she'd wanted to do was to make sure the woman was okay, but now she was running for her life...

As the night seemed to get darker, the sound of her pursuer confused her. She couldn't tell what direction the sounds came from. Disoriented, she couldn't find her car. Startled when she found herself at a dead end street that lead to an old cemetery, she barely suppressed the urge to cry. Since she didn't have her phone and chances of finding either a place to hide or a way out to a populated area, Margot made a quick decision to make her way through the cemetery. She had a vague recollection of seeing a cemetery downtown and if this was the one she thought it was, she figured she would find someone at the other side.

Darting into the darkness, she had a moment of fear of being in the land of the dead this late but shrugged it off. It was more important to get away from the murderer pursuing her than any ghost who may be about. She stumbled along. In a moment, she crashed into a tall monument. Reeling, she grabbed her head until the world stopped spinning. She held back her cry of pain but the world tilted in a weird way and tears streamed down her face. *Crap that hurt like crazy.*

Her panting breath was a giveaway to where she was. She kept moving, trying to hold her breath, and hit a shorter marker with her abdomen. She oofed out a sound and bit her tongue to keep from crying out.

Former medical examiner Margo Jenkins suspects that her sister was murdered. When her ex-brother-in-law's new wife dies in the same manner, Margo's suspicions are confirmed. Now she's on a quest to stop the man from murdering any more wives. But her quest is thwarted by local Pensacola, Florida, hot-shot homicide detective, Richard Higgins, who doubts her theories and attempts to rein her in. The only problem? This lady's not one to take direction well—even at the risk of her own safety…

Margot's sister, Margot is consumed with guilt and determined to stop the man before he can kill wife number three. Margot hires a private detective to locate her brother-in-law, who tracks him to Pensacola, Florida. But when she appeals to the Pensacola Police Department, the hot-shot homicide detective, sexy Richard Higgins scoffs at her theory—at first. But Margot is persuasive, and the detective reluctantly agrees to "look into it." Not satisfied with Richard's lukewarm response, Margot does some "looking into it" herself and is quickly in over her head and in hot water with the cops, the private detective she hired, and with the murder suspect himself. To complicate matters even further, there's the attraction between Richard and Margot—something that neither of them expected or wants. *Till Murder Do Us Part* is both a sweet romance and an intriguing mystery/thriller, a "who done it" with a twist. It will warm your heart while keeping you on the edge of your seat. ~ *Regan Murphy, Reviewer*

ACKNOWLEDGEMENTS

All of the places used in this novel are local, real places and ones that the author frequents. If you're ever in the area, try them out. They are all excellent. The author particularly recommends the restaurants for fine meals.

TILL MURDER DO US PART

Sherry Fowler Chancellor

A Black Opal Books Publication

This book is dedicated to my hometown, Pensacola, Florida, and all the people and places I love there.

CHAPTER 1

"Death is a debt we must all pay." ~ *Euripides,
Greek Tragedian, (c.480-406 BC)*

"My sister was the first to die," the lady said as she leaned across the beat up conference room table. Hands clasped together, she slid her arms forward, elbows scraping the metal edge of the surface.

"Are you here to confess to her murder?" Richard Higgins, a homicide detective with the Pensacola Police Department, asked. He had his leather portfolio open and pen poised to make notes. His captain sent for him when the blonde woman showed up at the precinct asking to speak to an officer who investigated murder cases. The type of person who came to the station unannounced with such a request was usually a nut job who wanted to confess to killing someone for some purpose—usually publicity or a misguided quest for fame.

This woman didn't look the part. She was nicely dressed as if she were a professional of some sort. The navy blue suit and obviously expensive shoes weren't the standard attire for a person who wanted to be known to the public as a criminal. Her haircut was also clearly not from the discount cutting place by the mall. The color of her eyes, a cornflower blue, distracted him, but only momentarily. Still leery, as it was never safe to assume anything in his line of work, Richard decided to play along and see where this was going.

"Let's start with your name, please," he said as he scribbled a bit on the page to be sure the pen worked.

"Margot Jenkins."

"All right then, Ms. Jenkins—"

"Miss."

"Excuse me?"

"It's *Miss* Jenkins. I've never been married."

Okay, so maybe she *was* a nut job. Wasn't that what he said? Richard leaned forward. "I thought that was what I said, ma'am."

"Well, no, you didn't. You said Ms. I don't like Ms."

"All righty then. miss it is. Now, can we get on with whatever brought you down here? Something about your sister, right?" Richard sat back, pulled the portfolio closer to his chest and prepared to make some notes.

"Like I said, my sister died first—"

"What was her name?"

"Geneva Murdock."

"I guess she was married? Since she has a different last name?" Richard wrote the name with a question mark behind it.

The woman tapped the tabletop with her right index finger. Expensive manicure. Richard knew these things as he had a high maintenance ex-wife. "Yes. She was married to Paul, my former brother-in-law who I think is involved with her death."

"What makes you say that?" Richard wrote down Paul Murdock. The name sounded familiar for some reason but he couldn't place it at the moment.

"My sister died ten years ago in Reno, Nevada—"

"That's out of my jurisdiction, *Miss* Jenkins."

"Do you ever let anyone finish a sentence? You've interrupted me at least four times in the less than five minutes I've been here. That's almost once a minute."

She pushed the metal chair back on the tiled floor, scraping the legs across the area. Richard's teeth clenched at the sound. He repressed the shudder but only barely.

Miss Jenkins stood.

"Sit down. My captain sent me in here to listen to what you have to say and—"

"And *now* you think you better take my statement? If I walk out of here and complain that you wouldn't let me tell you what I want to say, you'll be in trouble, right?"

Miss Jenkins still stood, her hand resting on the back of the chair.

Richard nodded at the chair. "Something like that, yes."

"Protecting your Internal Affairs file?"

She smiled. What Richard would call an evil, smug grin. She had him there, and she knew it. He'd have to follow orders or be prepared to explain why not.

"You could say that as well. Go on." He indicated the seat again with a tilt of the head. "Sit. Tell me how you think the PPD can assist you."

Miss Jenkins returned to her seat. "Ten years ago, my sister was found dead at her home, lying at the bottom of the inside staircase. She lived in Reno with her husband and was supposedly happy in her marriage."

"What was the official cause of death?" Richard was making notes, in case the woman followed through on her veiled threat to report that he wasn't paying her proper attention.

"The coroner said it was an accident."

"And you don't believe it?" Richard glanced up at her. She had an intense look on her face and seemed on the verge of tears. Great. He couldn't stand it when they cried. He shook his head. That wasn't completely true. After all, he did enjoy it when his questioning got so intense that he made a suspect confess or get teary but this was different. The lady seemed too fragile all of a sudden. He noticed her formerly steady hands were shaking.

"I wasn't entirely sold on the theory when it happened but since I wasn't there, I didn't get a chance to question it."

"Why would you have been in a position to do that?"

"I'm a trained medical examiner. I actually don't work in that field any longer, but I did for a year or two after I got out of medical school."

"So, how does this Reno ruling of accidental death get you to Pensacola and who was the next to die?" Richard scrawled a note about her past as an ME.

"I'm getting to that. Would you please allow me to tell this in my own way?"

"Sure, lady, I have all day. Take your time. I mean, after all, there's no other place I'd rather be than right here listening to you drag out this story for dramatic effect."

Richard knew by the look on her face that he'd probably gone too far with the sarcasm but couldn't she get to the heart of the matter sooner rather than later? He tilted his chair onto its two back legs and tossed his pen to the table.

"You must be one of the rudest men I've ever met." She stood again. "I'm going to get someone else who will take me seriously."

The front legs of Richard's chair hit the floor with a clunk. "I'm sorry. I'm testy. Come, sit. Tell me the rest."

She was really the testy one. Up and down out of her seat every time she got mad. It was as if he were in a room with a jack in the box.

"All right." The woman let out a deep sigh as she took her seat again. "This is your last chance, though. One more smart remark, and I'll be leaving as well as reporting your conduct."

It was Richard's turn to lean forward. "I hope you'll understand when I tell you that I'll give it my best effort not to wisecrack but since it's an integral part of my personality, I might slip up."

"Isn't integral a big word for you to be using? Above your pay grade, so to speak?"

The look on her face told him that she was trying to bait him into pushing her buttons again so she *could* leave the room. He didn't bite. Nope. Wasn't going there. "What happened next?" Richard picked up the pen.

"After my sister died, which like I said, was kind of mysterious to me, her husband kept their house for a year and a half or so but then started dating this woman named Jill Sikes. He had kept in touch with me during that period when he was supposedly mourning my sister. He called me when he put the home on the market. He told me that he was going to marry this Jill woman and she didn't want to live in the house where my sister had died."

"May I interrupt you for a moment?" Richard asked in what he thought was a respectful tone. Or he hoped so anyway.

"Yes." The woman smiled slightly. "And thank you for asking."

"Can you explain more about how your sister actually died? You said she fell going down a staircase, right?" He flipped back a page to glance at his notes.

"That's the thing. It appeared that way but it also seemed as if she could have fallen backward as she went *up* the wet staircase. It was hard to tell."

"Why was it wet?"

"My sister was a competitive swimmer as a teen and young woman. The house she and Paul lived in had a pool that was right outside a set of French doors that led inside to a teak spiral staircase to the upper floor. My sister was found in her swimsuit with her hair still damp. Her swim cap was on the floor at the foot of the stairs. Blood pooled around her head and the way she was lying there was a little off to me."

"What do you mean?" Richard was making notes again, even though the sister's case wasn't in his jurisdiction.

"I only saw the autopsy report and none of the crime scene photos so I can only go by the drawing on the report. It looked to me as if she were running up the stairs, slipped on a wet riser and fell backward. It may even be that she was running from an attacker as the French doors were open and there was no towel or anything to show that she had tried to dry off before entering the house. She was usually meticulous about that since the floor was ceramic tile and the staircase was wooden."

"Okay. So, I have a better picture now. Go on. You

were talking about a woman named Jill who was going to marry your brother-in-law."

"She *did* marry him and they were married for a while—I'm not sure how long—they moved away from Reno and I didn't hear from my brother-in-law again."

"Ever?"

"Well, not directly. I did recently hear that Jill died and that Paul is now living with another wife here in Pensacola. I'm afraid that he's going to kill her next."

"Whoa. Wait a second. What kind of leap is that? You're suspicious of whether or not your sister's death was an accident, you hear that this Jill lady died and now all of a sudden, this guy is a multiple murderer? I don't follow."

"Jill died by a fall down the stairs as well. How often, really, does someone actually die from a fall like that? Wouldn't they have contusions and bruising and maybe a subdural hematoma as opposed to dying?"

"I don't know, lady. I'm not an expert on falling."

"Come on, you're a homicide detective, aren't you? Think about it. How many deaths have you seen as a result of a fall down a staircase?"

Richard stopped to think about it for a moment. He'd been in the homicide division for five years and hadn't investigated even one such case.

He tapped the end of his pen on the note pad.

"You can't think of one, can you?" Miss Jenkins asked.

Or should he be thinking of her as doctor? Of course, she hadn't said doctor when she insisted on the miss.

"I confess, I can't, but that doesn't mean it hasn't happened."

"I also think it unlikely that two young wives of one guy die in the same manner. What are the odds of that?"

"First, how did you learn about this Jill's death and, second, let's say the Murdock guy did have something to do with both deaths, why would he think he could get away with the same manner of death more than once?"

"I got an online message from someone who knew my sister and also knew Jill before they moved away from Reno. This message stated that Jill and Paul moved to New Orleans and bought some kind of mansion there in the Garden District. The person said he or she thought he paid for it with the insurance money from Geneva's death."

"Who was the message from?" Richard prepared to write down the name.

"It was from a fake account. I tried to follow the trail back to see who contacted me but I ran into a dead end."

"Did you take it to a computer expert?"

"Not yet. I plan to. I was trying to get here in time to prevent another death. I have the laptop with me so if you know someone, I can use them."

"I'll see if one of our guys can look at it." Richard jotted a note about that. "What did you learn about Jill's death?"

"I took a day to go to the *Times Picayune* newspaper building and go through the archives. This girl fell down a flight of stairs in the home they owned—or should I say—he owned. It was titled in his name. There was a lot of blood but the coroner there also found that the death was an accident. I haven't been able to get a copy of that autopsy report but I did see a picture of the scene that someone at the paper took and it seemed to me that the amount of blood was way more than probable from a fall like that."

The woman's face was ashen and even though Richard didn't think she knew enough about the crime scene to make the leap to homicide, he got a vibe that she truly believed what she was saying.

"Did this same anonymous person tell you he lives in Pensacola now?"

"No. I found that out on my own." The woman had been making eye contact with Richard as she talked but now refused to look at him. She ran her well-manicured right index fingernail across one of the ruts on the tabletop. She studied it like it was the medical board she had to pass in order to practice medicine.

"How did you learn where he is?"

Still not glancing up at Richard, Miss Jenkins said, "I hired a private investigator."

"Is he the one who told you that your former brother in law is remarried yet again?"

She nodded.

"Where is this Murdock guy living?"

"In a house in Aragon. He paid cash for it. I think it was more insurance money."

"You *think*?"

She finally looked him in the eye. "I'm pretty sure. Yes."

"I find it odd that you suddenly seem less forthcoming. You were all gung-ho when you came in here, but now that I want to know why you're really here and how the PPD can help, you've gone coy on me."

"I can't imagine what you mean." The woman had the nerve to bat her eyelashes at him? Really? Did she think he was that easy to fool?

"I think you should tell me how you know these things like the life insurance being used to buy the home here and how you learned Murdock was remarried. I'm not sure what you hoped to accomplish by coming here today but, right now, I'm thinking you're trying to get the PPD on your side so you can exact your revenge on this poor slob you think may have harmed your sister. If you get us to believe he's some kind of wife-killing machine, you'll have free rein to kill him yourself and then claim self-defense."

Miss Jenkins leapt out of her chair so fast that the squeal of the legs on the tile that had previously caused Richard's teeth to gnash gave way instead to a thud as the whole thing landed on its back. She pointed at him and screeched, "You jerk. You'll pay for that."

With those words, she spun on the heel of what he presumed were five hundred dollar shoes and surged through the door, allowing it to slam closed. The sound reverberated through the room.

Richard sat back with a smile on his face. He'd told her. Sure, he was probably going to regret it when his captain got through with him, but her smug attitude needed shutting down. It was worth the write up on his personnel jacket.

⌘⌘⌘

Margot stalked out of the police station without stopping to talk to the arrogant detective's supervisor. She wanted to with all her soul but after the last moments of the meeting with Richard Higgins, she realized that she could very well be in legal trouble herself with the methods she'd used to track Paul Murdock to Pensacola. It was hard for her not to report the officer's insubordination and rudeness, but she needed to protect herself from any charges.

At a loss what to do next, she got in her car and drove away from the police station on Hayne Street and made her way to Cervantes Street and the Coffee Cup. She'd grab a lunch special at the counter there and see if she could reach the investigator/hacker she'd hired to get his thoughts on her next move. She'd only been in town a few days but when a local recommended the diner to her, she ate there and loved it. Today she knew she would find the comfort foods of meat and potatoes it offered to be the perfect thing to ease her wounded pride. Wheeling in to the parking lot behind the place, she was surprised to find several local police cars there.

She got out of the car, hoping it was a favorite lunch place for the cops and there was not a crime in progress. Since the place was so close to the station, she presumed it was the first option. Shrugging and taking a chance they were open for business, she went in and found a place at the counter to sit. There was a table near the door with four police officers seated there. She nodded at them as she sat. Yep, had to be a cop hangout.

Pulling out her phone, Margot inhaled the smell of the delicious food cooking. It was fried chicken day, for sure, since that was the aroma permeating the air. She ordered the special with lima beans and collard greens. While she waited, she sent a text message to her investigator to meet her after lunch at Plaza Ferdinand. She closed her eyes and relived the meeting with the detective. In retrospect, she'd played it all wrong. She should have been friendly and calm, instead of letting him push her buttons. Her temper had gotten her in trouble more than once.

When she arrived at the grassy park on Palafox Street, Margot immediately noticed the investigator, Mike "Mitch" Mitchell seated on one of the benches facing the obelisk in the middle of the park. He was hard to miss since he wore a fedora as if he were a PI from the 1930s or something. It was an odd affectation, but he was so good at his job, Margot didn't let it bother her. She'd found him online and even though he was based in New Orleans, he was familiar with the Florida gulf coast area as well.

Walking toward him, she watched as he fed a few pigeons that gathered around his feet. Why would he be feeding those rodents with wings? They carried all kinds of disease and she planned to set him straight on why he needed to stop encouraging them to be around people.

Before she arrived at the bench, Mitch turned his head toward her. "Good afternoon. What's up?"

"How'd you hear me on the grass? I thought I was being quiet."

He laughed. "Can't sneak up on me. I have eyes in the back of my head."

Margot took a seat beside the man and handed him a container. "Bull. I don't know how you did it but my mother always said the same thing."

"Mammas always say that."

"And, apparently, so do private eyes."

"We do, indeed. How did the meeting at the PPD go, and what did you bring me?"

"It's a piece of lemon pie. I thought you might enjoy it. The meeting was not so great."

"Who'd you get? Who was on duty?"

"Some jackass named—"

"Let me guess, Richard Higgins?"

"How'd you know?"

"As soon as you said jackass, it was all over." Mitch laughed so hard he almost choked. When he recovered, he said, "Been up against that ole boy before. He wouldn't know me by sight as I stayed in the background in that situation but he was pretty tough to my associates in that case."

"He didn't look that old to me."

"He's in his thirties but I meant it as ole boy as in long time resident of the area with a family connections going back to the founding of the town."

"Oh." Margot nodded. "Got it. The old boy network. Great. That's just great."

"It'll be okay. He's bright. He might have given you a hard time today but he's like that proverbial dog with a bone. If you planted the seed the right way, Rick will dig and dig until he gets to the truth. You'll see."

"I bolted when he started asking how we traced Paul here. I got scared."

"Leave him to me. If he gets a burr up his rear over it, I'll talk to him. Just don't tell him I hacked into Murdock's computer by tracing his email address."

"I didn't tell him anything. He doesn't know who I hired."

Mitch tossed out some more pieces of bread from his bag to the pigeons. "Higgins will figure it out. If he cares about the matter, that is. If you whet his appetite, he'll be all about the meal. He loves a mystery and I hope you gave him one that made him curious."

"I hope I did, too." Margot touched Mitch's hand. "Please stop feeding those nasty things."

"They're not nasty. They need love too."

Margot stood. "Lord save me from a lover of plague-carrying vermin."

"Even vermin have mammas, Margot Jenkins."

"And fathers, it seems, Mitch." She grinned. "It seems I can't change your mind about feeding them, but if you get bubonic plague, don't call me."

"I won't. Where did you decide to stay? In case I need you?"

"I'm at the Hampton on the beach."

"Nice choice."

"Thanks. I'll call you later." Margot returned to her car while Mitch continued to feed the birds. She watched him for a few moments, then drove away headed toward Aragon Court to do a drive-by of Paul Murdock's house on her way out to the beach. Luckily, it was right on the way.

∽∾∽∾

After the annoying woman left, Richard spoke to his captain about her allegations. He tried his best to blow off all she said as nonsense, but since there were no active homicides pending at the moment, the captain insisted they at least look into the situation to see if there was any truth to what she said. Thinking it was a colossal waste of time, Richard pulled up some internet sites on his computer and searched for articles related to the death of the woman in Reno as well as the woman in New Orleans.

The more he read, the more intrigued Richard became. Maybe the lady wasn't loony tunes after all. There was a lot to consider by reading between the lines on the news stories as reported. Richard had experience with newspapers and how the journalists who covered the crime beat tried to say as much as they could get away with but dancing around other things—things that maybe the investigator or the prosecutor alluded to but couldn't actually have on the record. The articles he read were leading him to believe there was more here that wasn't disclosed than was.

Richard printed a few of the most intriguing articles, packed them into a file folder, and left the precinct. He headed down Gregory Street to the local library. He wanted to check out some books on psychology. He'd been to a class at the FBI headquarters in Quantico on criminal profiling, and he wanted to grab a few volumes to refresh his memory on the things he'd learned there.

Parking on the street, he entered the newly remodeled building. Glancing around, he was taken anew by the beauty of the sunlight shining through the large, rounded windows with the mullions. He appreciated the way the prisms of glass seemed to twinkle with the heat of the rays beating down through the clear surface. Since they'd redone the library with the mahogany shelves and the old railway clock, it seemed to Richard that the city was moving into a brand new architectural era. The downtown historical district had always had a strict policy on how the buildings could be renovated and presented. This seemed to be stretching outward into other areas of town, which was more than okay with him.

He spent fifteen or twenty minutes perusing the stacks for the books he wanted. Once he had them amassed, Richard stood in line to check them out. As he handed his selections to the librarian, someone called his name.

The blonde woman grinned at Richard as she stepped up to stand beside him at the checkout desk. "What are you doing here? Aren't you supposed to be saving the world from crime?"

"Even superheroes need a break, Janette."

"Please don't disillusion me, my friend." She tilted her head to read the spines of the books as the librarian handed them across the counter. She read them out loud. "*When lovers Kill, Inside the Mind of a Serial Killer, Husbands Who Murdered Their Wives,* and *Till Murder Do Us Part.*" Janette glanced up at Richard and back at the titles.

A half-smile played on her lips. "Is this light weekend reading or is there something going on in this town that I need be educated about?"

"Nothing for sure. Just something I wanted to research."

With books in hand, he walked toward the exit but Janette wasn't going to make it easy for him to leave without satisfying her curiosity.

She followed alongside him. "The fact that you said 'nothing for sure' piques my interest, Detective. I haven't heard any rumors of any kind of serial killer on the loose. In fact, there hasn't even been a homicide here in a couple of months. The last two were drug related in Brownsville and you caught both of those guys, so I fail to see what this is about." She slapped her forehead. "Is it one of the cold cases you're looking into? What made you think it's a serial killer?"

Exasperated, Richard stopped in the middle of the parking lot. "Can you let it go? For once?"

"You know I can't do that. What kind of reporter would I be if I let go the fact that Pensacola's leading homicide dick is reading up on serial killers? Ones that appear to be married? Isn't that usually *not* the case? Aren't they normally loners?"

"Good grief, you're relentless, aren't you?"

"You already knew that, Richard."

"I did but I also know that, eventually, you'll give up. When the door is slammed in your face enough times, you'll walk away."

Tears welled in her eyes. "That's not fair. That's a low blow, and you *know* I didn't want to walk away. I only did so that everyone's sanity could be saved. I'd be back in a second if I thought it would work out. You know that, too."

With his free hand, Richard reached out to Janette. When he touched her, she recoiled as if he'd slapped her. "I'm sorry, J. That *was* a low blow. I shouldn't have brought all that up."

"It's never far from the surface, anyway. I wasn't going to ask about it but now that you've broached the subject, I *have* to know. How is he?"

Her face had gone so pale, Richard was afraid she would collapse on the pavement.

"Come over here in the shade. I don't want you to pass out and hit your head." Richard led Janette under the closest tree. He set the books on the ground at his feet.

Janette leaned against the tree with her hands behind her back resting on the bark. "Is he adjusting to being home?"

God, he didn't want to talk about this. His former police partner and roommate had been shot in a home invasion robbery when the two of them had still been on patrol. His best friend was now paralyzed from the waist down and had recently moved back to their house in East Hill from his stint in rehab learning to adjust to life in a wheelchair.

Richard ran his hand over his eyes before answering her. He relived that moment of the shooting in that split second.

"Philip seems to be adjusting all right. He's able to get

around the house. I had the countertops lowered while he was gone and that seems to help. I built a ramp as well. He's doing fine physically."

"And emotionally?"

The anguish in her voice wrenched at Richard's heart. He shook his head ruefully. "Not so hot. Sorry."

The tears flowed down her cheeks. "I wish I could make him understand—"

"I'm afraid he never will. It's sad, hon, I know, but he's adamant that he can't bring you down with him. I've asked and asked him to let you at least come by and see him, but it's not going to happen. He's pretty stubborn as you know."

Janette wiped her tears on the back of her hand. "I love him, Richard. I don't know how to prove that I want him with or without the ability to walk. I want to be with him. As long as he's still alive, I want to be part of his life."

"I know you do but he can't see past his own anger right now so we have to leave it alone for the moment. I hope someday he will come around, but you need to realize that he may never do so and get on with your life."

"Easy for you to say. I'd feel like I'm abandoning him if I moved on."

"Please don't hold back for him. If you do, you may find you've let your life pass you by." Richard leaned over to pick up the books. "I need to get going but do you want to go to lunch one day next week? We can talk then."

"Let's do that and we can compare notes on letting life pass us by because aren't you doing the same thing? You're not fooling anyone yourself, mister. It's well known all over the city that Richard Higgins blames himself for his partner, Philip Segars being in a wheelchair. The detective does nothing but solve crimes and take target practice as if he could atone for his sins by being super-cop." She shoved herself off the tree and whirled around to stalk away. Over her shoulder, she called out, "I'm going to figure out what you're doing with those books, too. Look for my story on it in the paper."

Richard shook his head. Janette was correct. She would find out what he was doing as she was dogged in her pursuit of a story once she scented one, and she was also right about his guilt about Philip. He didn't think he could live his own life while the man he loved as a brother was so miserable in his.

Richard returned to his car, tossed the books on the passenger seat, and slid behind the wheel. He drove away and to the firing range. His second trip of the day. Yes, Janette was definitely right about the guilt.

CHAPTER 2

"The ocean is a mighty harmonist." ~ William Wordsworth, English poet (1770-1850)

Dawn at the beach was the second most beautiful time of the day. Margot realized that as she took a morning run on the wet sand. She tried to run on the dry area of the beach but the sand was so thick and soft that her feet sank in and bogged her down, so she moved down to the breakwater. It was so lovely with the first shades of pink in the sky seeming to float across the greenish blue water and up to the sugar-white sands.

The evening before, Margot sat out on the deck of the hotel near the tiki bar and watched the sun go down. It was a spectacular sight—almost like a fire in the sky.

She'd heard that term before but never really knew what it meant until she witnessed it. Sure, she'd seen sunsets before but there was something special about that one, with the smell of the salt water in her nose and the sound of the seagulls cawing overhead. She sipped her cocktail and wished her sister were with her. Of course, if Geneva were there, she'd probably be either in the pool or the ocean. That girl sure did love to swim.

Thinking about her sister's love of competitive swimming reminded Margot anew of why she was in the area in the first place. She finally left the patio of the hotel and went up to bed. Now, this morning, she ran along the shore with her mind on what she needed to do next. She regretted her march out of the police station the day before and knew she would have to swallow her pride and return to the precinct. She only hoped that snarky detective wouldn't require her to grovel too much before he agreed to assist her.

Finally ready to return to the hotel and make herself ready for the day, Margot reversed course and headed back down the beach. Once in front of her lodgings, she ran across the looser sand farther from the shore and up to the green lounging chairs that the hotel staff were setting out for the day's use by the patrons. In the last one sat a man in a pair of khaki slacks and a navy blue polo shirt. He wore mirrored sunglasses and seemed to be watching her progress up the beach.

From a distance, it was hard to tell who he was, but

she thought it might have been that detective from yesterday. The man had the same curly hair and body build, as far as she could tell since he was stretched out in the chair, but she wouldn't know for sure until he either took off the glasses so she could see his sky-blue eyes or until he opened his sarcastic mouth, whichever came first. She chuckled under her breath at that thought. She'd bet it was the sarcasm that would win out.

As she arrived at the occupied chair, the man stood and whipped the glasses off his face. He held them by one stem and with his free hand, he reached out to shake hers. "Remember me?"

It *was* the detective and he actually smiled. His eyes sparkled almost as much as the sun's rays on the ocean. The smile was quite breathtaking. Margot thought it was a good thing he didn't dazzle her with that secret weapon yesterday as she might have melted into a puddle at his feet.

"Indeed I do remember you, Detective Higgins. Did you drive all the way out here to the beach and pay the toll so you could tell me again how wrong I am about my former brother-in-law?"

"On the contrary, I came to talk to you about the research I've been doing and to pick your brain some about your sister's death. Can I treat you to breakfast?"

"I'll need a shower first. Do you have time to wait?"

"I do. I'll sit out on the deck and enjoy the sunshine until you're ready. How's that?"

"I'll be quick. I don't want to hold you up." Margot pulled the elastic out of her hair and ran her hands through the curls as she led the way to the beachside door leading into the hotel.

He sat at one of the tables with the umbrella up to shade the area from the sun. "Take your time. I'll be here."

Margot turned to face him with her hand on the door. "I thought you were going to soak up the sun? What's with sitting in the shade?"

"As a Florida native, I know to take it easy in the sun, especially when it's going to be a scorcher later today. It's nice to keep cool while I can. A bit of shade isn't the end of the world, even though some of you northern folks think if you're in Florida you need to be baking your-selves to a shade of lobster red."

"You think I'm from the north?"

"Yep. You are."

"I didn't think I had an accent."

"Sure you do. Everyone has a bit of language that gives away where they're from."

Margot crossed her right ankle over her left and leaned against the doorjamb. "If you know so much, where do you think I live?"

"I didn't say *live*. I said where you come from." He grinned and again, his eyes lit up. If she didn't know bet-ter, she'd think he was flirting with her.

"Then where am I from?"

Richard waved his hand in a casual way toward the lobby. "This isn't getting your shower taken."

"You're going to have to answer sooner or later." She took a step inside.

He called out, "You're from Ohio and live now in California."

Shocked, she gaped at him. He was right. How could he know either of those things?

"Go. Go." Richard waved his hand again. "I'm getting too hungry. It'll be way past breakfast time if you don't hurry."

She entered the hotel and headed to her room on the second floor by the elevator. She always asked for that room in hotels since she liked to be near the exit. She normally traveled alone and didn't like to carry her gear a long way.

Taking a fast shower, she dressed in a dark green knit dress with a ruched bodice and a skirt that hit her right at the knee. She wore a pair of white sandals and pulled her hair up in a bun as she normally wore it. Deciding against the pantyhose since they'd almost suffocated her the day before in the summer heat, she made sure she had plenty of the SPF 15 moisturizer on her arms and legs. She also added some to her face before she applied her light coating of makeup. The cop was right. The sun was definitely different here than what she was used to.

Back in the lobby, Margot was surprised to see Richard chatting with a man with a broom next to the sofa in the center of the space. The man leaned on the handle of the broom and seemed intent on the conversation.

When Richard noticed her, he shook the man's hand and walked toward her.

"Ready to go? There's a great local place for breakfast. It's called the Coffee—"

"Cup?" Margot laughed as she finished his sentence.

"I take it you've been there, then?" He placed his hand on her elbow as he escorted her out the automatic double doors and into the sloping parking lot.

"I had lunch there yesterday. It seems to be a hangout for the boys in blue."

"It is. It's an old Pensacola institution and very popular. It's been around since the 1940s. Sometimes there's a line to get in and, if so, we'll go over to Krispy Kreme instead since everyone knows all cops like donuts, right?"

"I'm not stereotyping law enforcement. I happened to notice yesterday that there were several patrol cars in the parking lot and several officers eating inside." Geez the man sure was sensitive about his fellow cops.

"I'm only kidding. You know it's kind of hard to joke around with someone as serious as you seem to be. Do you ever lighten up?" He led her toward a dark brown sedan. "This is me."

"I've always been subdued and quiet. I *do* have a sense of humor, though I don't believe that it's appropriate to laugh and joke around when I'm trying to prevent someone else from dying."

"Whoa, ho." Richard held his hands up in front of his face. "What do you mean prevent someone else from dying? I thought we were looking into the deaths of your sister and Jill Sikes. I can't agree to let you do anything to approach the man or his current wife." Richard opened the passenger side door for her and she slid in.

"You can't really stop me, either. Let's say I want to befriend her and warn her about her husband. What can you do to prevent that? It's not a crime."

Leaning on the top of the door, he looked down at her. "I can only warn you against it. If the man is as dangerous as you say, you're messing around with your own life. I can't say that's a very bright idea for someone who must be smart, what with the medical degree and all that." The detective shut the door and walked around the front of the vehicle to the driver's side.

Once he was seated with his seatbelt fastened, she turned to look at his profile. "Are you telling me that you'd always want to be on the wrong side of death? To solve murders rather than prevent them?"

"The wrong side of death? I've never heard it put that way before. I'm a homicide detective. That's what I do. I solve deaths. Sure, I'd love to prevent them—to work myself out of a job, so to speak—but that's not going to happen. At least not in this lifetime."

"But if you could, wouldn't you?"

"There you go with that persistence again." Richard turned the key in the ignition and once the motor roared to life, he put the car in reverse and backed out of the parking space. He drove down the beach road and out to the toll bridge in silence.

As he entered the town between the beach and Pensacola, Gulf Breeze, Margot couldn't stay quiet any longer. "Isn't persistence a good thing?"

"It *can* be, but when it's taken to extremes, it can be dangerous as opposed to a positive trait."

"Listen. I get what you're saying. I do."

"Why do I sense that there's a but in there?"

"Because there is."

"Somehow I knew that." Richard sighed. "What?"

"While I'd love to take down the man who killed my sister, I'm also a realist. We may not be able to do that since so much time has passed. I understand it's an uphill battle but I also know that I don't want to leave some other unsuspecting woman in a position of peril. I think she at least has the right to know she's in danger."

"You don't think she already knows her husband has two dead wives?"

"I have no clue. I haven't spoken to the man in years. I can bet, though, if she knows about them, he's fed her some line of crap about what happened."

"Tell me this then, what makes you think she'll believe what *you* have to say? First, you're a stranger to her and, second, as soon as you tell her you're the sister of wife number one, she's going to be suspicious of your motives."

Richard wheeled into a parking spot behind the Coffee Cup.

"Why would she be suspicious of that?"

"Depending on what Paul Murdock told her, she could think you're the disgruntled sister-in-law who doesn't want him to be happy. With your sister dead, you could be someone who wants him to grieve forever and be miserable that he's found some happiness with another woman."

"Really? You think that?"

"I don't myself but I'm trying to make you understand that the man has either *not* told his new wife about his past marriages or, if he has, he's sold her a bill of goods and she's not going to take your word against his." He opened his door. "Come on. I'm starving."

They walked around the side of the building and joined the small line. It took about ten minutes for them to be seated. Once they were in a corner booth with menus in hand, Richard picked up the conversation. "I don't know if you've ever been married but when people are in a position of trust—and marriage is the deepest relationship of trust since the two people share such strong intimacy—it's hard for an outsider to affect the depth of that trust. Do you understand what I'm trying to say?"

"Not to be crass, Detective, but is what you're alluding to the fact that once two people have had sex, that it's impossible to come between them and convince one of them that the other is a murderer?"

The waitress picked the moment Margot uttered the words *two people have sex* to arrive to take their orders. The server quirked her eyebrows at Richard. "Would you like some biscuits and gravy with your sex, Detective Higgins?"

"Very funny, Sarah. Bring me my usual." He handed the menu to the waitress.

Sarah turned to Margot and winked. "And you, ma'am? Now that you have the detective right where I've always wanted him, what will you have?"

"I'm afraid you misunderstood the conversation—" Margot started to say.

"Never mind, Miss Jenkins. Sarah is an old friend. One who thinks that gives her the right to annoy people. Go ahead and order. Don't try to explain anything."

"What if she does something to my food? She seems interested in you and I need to be sure she knows that I'm not a threat."

Richard glanced up at Sarah. "Oops, sorry. I keep forgetting this one has no sense of humor. Everything is serious. No teasing allowed."

"Oh, well then, miss, I know you're not a real threat then. Richard only dates women he can make laugh. If he can't make you giggle, he's not interested, so there's no need for me to mess around with your food. What'll you have?"

Sarah smiled and held out her order pad with her pencil poised to take Margot's order.

"Oh, yeah, and always make sure you call her miss, Sarah. No ms. for this lady. She has an aversion to the title." Richard winked.

"Good grief. You're impossible." Margot turned to the waitress. "I'll take the pancake special with two slices of bacon on the side."

"Very well." Sarah jotted the order down and sashayed to the kitchen.

As soon as she was gone, Margot said, "To get back to our conversation, I haven't ever been married but I think I understand the concept of intimacy."

"In a clinical, medical way?"

"Why do you say it that way? You don't know anything about me or my past or the way I think."

"You said you're a doctor. I think you look at a lot of life in a sterile way. That's what I've observed in the time I've known you." Richard played with his fork. "Guess what? I have news for you. Life is messy and doesn't always work out the way we want it to."

"Look, obviously you've formed an erroneous opinion of me, and maybe I've done the same for you. It seems you wanted to talk to me about something since you invited me to breakfast. Shouldn't we get around to whatever that was and forget the personal opinions of each other?"

Sarah returned with their food and placed a plate in front of each of them. The waitress didn't say a word but she grinned at Richard.

Once Sarah walked away, Richard pulled out his note-pad. "I made a few notes last night after copying some articles I found on the Internet. I read through the reports I could find online and it seems to me that some things in both deaths could still use some investigation. I know you said you wanted to see the autopsy report on Jill Sikes but I also think we need to get the crime scene photos from both your sister's case and Ms. Sikes's. I'm going to give my chief a nudge to see if he can make some calls to the other police departments or sheriff's offices and get our hands on these items. I'm going to have to convince him it's likely we'll find something to move forward on. Do you have any ideas how I can do that?"

಄಄಄

It seemed like the woman would never get her syrup poured just right. Richard sensed Margot's reluctance to speak as she delayed her response to him. He waited patiently for her to decide that her breakfast was perfectly aligned on her plate before he cleared his throat loudly twice.

If that didn't convince her to break her silence, he'd have to think of something else.

Margot pierced a bit of the pancake with her fork. "Will you stop staring at me?"

"Are you going to answer my question? How are we going to convince the chief to get the information we need or are you ready to quit the moment anyone questions you?"

"You're not giving me a chance to think it through and make a good argument. Push, push, push is all you do."

"It's how I'm wired, lady. That's one of the reasons I'm in the job I'm in. I have a great clearance rate on the cases I handle."

"I'm glad to hear it but can you let me think while I eat?"

"I thought it was only men who couldn't multi-task." Richard cut up his open-faced biscuits smothered with red-eye gravy. The scent of the ham on his plate wafted up and made his stomach growl.

"Thinking while eating isn't multi-tasking."

"I meant you couldn't *talk* and eat but I guess you shouldn't anyway since grandma said never talk with your mouth full." He nodded at her plate. "Eat. I won't speak until your plate is empty."

They ate in surprisingly companionable silence. Richard tried to figure out the woman while he enjoyed his food. She seemed to be bright and had to be intelligent in order to have a medical degree, but she also was an enigma to him. Every person he ever knew who had gone to medical school insisted on being called doctor and she had a thing about being called miss. What was that all about? It seemed the lady had some mystery about her, in addition to the mystery surrounding her dead sister. He hated to admit it but he was as intrigued by her as well as the cases she wanted him to investigate.

Finally, Margot's plate was empty. Sarah immediately came over with the check. Richard knew he was expected to get up and go pay at the front. The waitresses wanted the tables turned fast so they could maximize their tips. He nodded to Margot. "We can finish the conversation at the station."

"No hanging out over coffee?"

"Nope. Gotta move. You'll see when we get outside how the line has grown while we ate. Come on. Time to clear out." Richard stood, pulling his wallet out as he made his way past the tables to the cash register, waving at some of the other locals he knew.

When he arrived at the cash register, Margot handed him some cash for her meal. Richard tried to shake it off but she shoved it into his hand. "Sorry. This isn't a date. I pay my own way."

"Do you *ever* relax?" He shook his head. Man, this chick was so tightly wound he was surprised she didn't spin off like a tornado across the plains. He'd never seen anyone so rigid. He idly wondered what could have made her that way but then shrugged it off. Not his business.

She smiled. "I admit freely that I'm intense but I do sometimes take a day off."

"That was *almost* a joke, right?"

Margot shook her head. "Come on. Let's go sell your chief on getting us those autopsy pictures and the report from Sikes's death."

He led her to his car and then drove them to the station, where they parked then headed inside to the chief's office to see when he would be available to have a chat.

As luck would have it, the chief had just finished with a meeting with one of the local city councilwomen and was showing her out as Richard and Margot walked past his office. The chief nodded at them. "Detective."

"Sir." Richard returned the greeting. "I was just going to ask Madge if you had time at some point today to meet with me and Miss Jenkins. She has a multi-jurisdictional problem and we thought maybe you could help."

The chief glanced at his wrist. "I have about ten minutes right now. Come on in." He pivoted on his heel and passing his assistant, said to her, "I'll be with Detective Higgins for the next few minutes."

"Don't forget your meeting with the mayor."

"I know. I'll be out in time to ride over to city hall. I won't be late—" The chief glanced back at Richard. "—will I, Detective?"

"Not on my watch, sir." Richard followed the chief and stepped aside to allow Margot to enter the room ahead of him.

The room was spare. A couple of old leather beat up chairs sat in front of a wooden desk that could be purchased at any local office supply store. The chief's chair was a rolling one and sported the same color upholstery as the others.

The chief sat in his spot and indicated the other seats.

"Sit. I don't have long. What can I do to help you, Miss…uh…Jenkins, right?"

"That's right." She nodded. "I'm trying to stop a murder—"

The chief leaned forward in his seat, elbows on his desk. "What?"

Richard held his right hand up. "Hold on. Let me do this."

"I don't see why I can't tell the chief as well as you can." Margot huffed at the end of her sentence.

"He already said he has no time so let me be succinct. I can do that faster than you telling the whole story again."

The chief looked at the watch on his arm again. He tapped on the face with his index finger. "Time's ticking, Higgins. What do you need from me specifically?"

"Two phone calls. We need copies of autopsy reports as well as photos from New Orleans and from Reno. We think there's a man who may have killed two wives and now he's here in Pensacola with another wife."

"Are you sure? This isn't some fishing expedition, is it?"

At the same time Margot said, "No," Richard said, "Maybe."

She gaped at the detective and he noticed, not for the first time, how the area around the base of her throat became a blotchy red when she was upset. He made a mental note to keep an eye open for that in the future.

Miss Jenkins pouted. "Why'd you say that? Now he's not going to help us since you said you were only guessing if the reports would lead somewhere."

"I'm never going to keep the truth from my boss, lady. My integrity won't allow me to do that, and I certainly wouldn't risk my career over this case. Or non-case, whatever it turns out to be." Richard knew he was probably being unfair to her since she had so much emotion invested in the outcome but he was clear-eyed and focused, and he truly wasn't sure there was anything out there to find against the Murdock man.

"Stop." The chief stood. "You've used your time and I need to be on my way. Higgins, leave me the information on who I need to call and what matter we need records on. I don't mind making the calls, but that's all I'm going to do unless something else comes to light after we get the initial reports." He held his hand out to Margot. "I hope whatever you're looking to accomplish happens. I can see your passion but I have to warn you—Detective Higgins is pretty straight-laced and that's what makes him important to this department. He won't let you lead him astray, and you're better off not trying to make him conform to what you desire."

Richard was glad to see that the woman didn't try to argue with the chief. She'd gotten what she wanted—the promise of the phone calls—but she'd been so pushy thus far he thought for a moment she was going to blow it by pressing for more.

He almost wanted to say *good girl* but he refrained.

"Thank you, sir. I appreciate any help your department is willing to offer." Margot held her hand out and the chief shook it.

"I really must go now," he said as he exited his office, leaving Richard and Margot alone.

She turned to Richard. "That went well."

"Never again try to make me look bad to my superior. Do you understand?"

"I don't know why you're so up in arms about it. The man clearly thinks you're the most important thing to happen to the Pensacola Police Department in the last millennium."

"Just don't do it again." He turned and strode out of the room.

಄಄಄

Margot couldn't believe how angry Detective Higgins was. They'd gotten what they wanted from the chief and she would soon be able to review the pictures and see for herself how the bodies were found. She shuddered a little at the thought of having to dispassionately look over her sister's death photos, but she knew she had to do it if she wanted justice for Geneva.

Following the detective out of the chief's office, Margot was surprised to see Richard was leading her out of the building again. She thought they might sit in the conference room and talk but it seemed the man wanted her gone. Once outside, standing on the curb, she touched him on the upper arm. The rock-hard upper arm. "Are you going to be mad at me forever now?"

"I'm sorry to say that's a distinct possibility." He held up his hand. "Before you go on and I see by your face that you have more to say, let me tell you this. I don't plan to hold a grudge about what you did in the chief's office but I think, based on the history of our dealings thus far, that I will probably end up mad at you again and more than once, I'm afraid."

"Somehow, I don't think you're afraid of anything."

"You have *no* idea." He shook his head. "Now, I need to take you to your hotel so I can get some work done today."

"I'll call a cab."

"No, that's going to cost you a bit. I don't mind driving you."

"I have a friend who's nearby. I'll call him to come get me. You go on and leave that information on your boss's desk so we can get those reports. That's more important than getting me to the hotel."

"If you're sure. I really don't mind taking you."

Margot pulled her phone from her purse. "See? I'm dialing now."

Richard shook his head and opened the door to the station. "I'll call you when I have the paperwork."

"Thanks."

He went inside and she finished her call to Mitch. She wanted to do another drive-by of the house in Aragon and she was sure that Mitch would be up for it. He was one man who did as she asked. Of course, she *was* paying him.

In a few moments, Mitch came whipping into the parking lot on two wheels in his burnt-orange-colored Nissan Rogue. Margot thought it was an odd vehicle choice for a man who seemed so like a detective from an old Dashiell Hammett novel. He was an enigma, for sure, with his hacking abilities as well as his deductive skills. He was brilliant at his job. Mitch pulled to a stop in front of where she still stood on the step of the police station.

Opening the car door, Margot slid in to the passenger seat. "Seems to me you're awfully brave to scoot in here over the speed limit what with all the cops hanging around."

"The day I'm afraid of some traffic cop is the day I turn in my PI license. Not my driver's license, mind you." Mitch pulled off his fedora and wiped his brow. Replacing the hat and wheeling out on to Hayne Street at the same time, he glanced at her. "Where to?"

"I want to swing by the Aragon house and see if we can see if either Paul or his wife are home."

"I'm not sure about that, Margot. What if he *is* home? What are you going to do, knock on the door and ask him if he's killed anyone lately?"

"Of course not. That would be insane."

"*I* know that but I wasn't sure if *you* did. It's also going to alert him to a possible problem if he sees you. We don't want to spook him and, if you pass by in broad daylight, he could very well spot you and then it's all over. He may run again and bury himself deep where you can't find him."

"If he doesn't change his name, we'll be able to locate him anywhere he goes."

"I'm not sure we can rely on my hacker skills over and over. It could get hairy if we press our luck where that's concerned. I'd rather your former brother-in-law stays put and thinks he's in the clear for what he's done in the past. That gives us time to properly investigate everything and then when we have all the evidence we need, we move in for the kill." He grinned over at her. "So to speak."

"I understand the concept of wanting him to think he's safe and hoping he'll let down his guard. I'm also impatient and actually have a crazy desire to confront him so I can see his face when he finds out that I'm determined to prove he killed my sister and that other poor woman who was stupid enough to marry him."

Mitch turned down Ninth Avenue headed toward the Aragon neighborhood near the bay front. "I'm thinking I need to lock you away so you don't blow this whole thing in your enthusiasm to get the man to the electric chair. I certainly hope after all you've done to try to get justice for your sister that you don't muck it up now."

"I won't. I know it's important to keep a low profile

and I promise to keep to the shadows. If Paul is in the yard or comes out of his house, I'll duck. He won't see me."

"Get ready then. Almost there." They neared the road to Paul Murdock's house and Mitch turned on his signal to indicate the right turn. They traveled slowly down the street, past two people on bicycles and three kids walking a dog. "I get that these houses are nice, but they sure are on top of their neighbors," he said. "What if you absolutely hate the guy next door? There's only a few feet between their walls than yours. Can you imagine?"

She shuddered. "I can't even begin to fathom it. I hear these places sell for over half a million dollars. For that, I'd want some room to roam."

"I guess your former brother-in-law doesn't care about that kind of thing."

"Sadly, I think the only thing he looks for in a house is a second floor and a staircase." A small sob escaped from Margot's lips.

"I know." Mitch reached over and patted her leg. He tapped the brakes. "Quick, duck down. I see a car coming out of his driveway."

"Crap." She slid toward the floorboard and hunched over as Mitch moved closer to Murdock's house.

Margot heard the other car pass them going in the opposite direction. Once it was gone, she sat up. "Was it him?"

"No. It was two women."

"Was one of them his wife?"

"The driver looked like the picture of her. I have no idea who the other was."

"What kind of car was it?"

"Black Volvo. Tan interior."

"That's her, right? Based on what you found out before I got here?"

"They actually have *two* black Volvos. One is a 2009 and the other is a 2012. I never heard of both partners in a marriage having the same car. How do they tell them apart unless there was a manufacturer's change in body type from one year to the next?"

"I imagine they can, based on the junk in them." Margot couldn't resist laughing as she recalled all the things her sister used to keep in her car. The laughter was tinged with a bit of sorrow since Geneva was gone but it was nice to think of her for a moment with a smile.

"What's that mean?" Mitch continued down the street to the end of the block. "Want me to drive by again?"

"Yeah. See if the other car is there."

He made a U-turn and headed in the direction from which they'd come. "What did you mean by junk kept in the car?"

"Don't be silly. Surely you know? Look around here in your own vehicle. There's a small blanket in the seat behind me and a plaid umbrella in the seat behind you. If you were married, do you think your wife would have the exact same things in hers and in the same place?"

"No, but I still wouldn't want matching cars and boring black Volvos at that."

"Good point." They were next to the house Murdock owned. No other signs of life were around. Margot was disappointed as she wanted to get a glimpse of the man after all the years that had gone by. She wondered if he still was handsome and charming. Truth be known, she'd been a little jealous when her sister landed the gorgeous blond man as her spouse. Now, of course, Margot was grateful that she hadn't gotten him for herself but she sure wished Geneva had been able to get safely away from him.

"Since we don't know where Murdock is, don't you think we need to move off his street before he comes home?"

"I agree," she said. "What's next?"

"I think it's time we take a trip out to the place where Murdock works and see if we can spot his car. I'd like to establish what his routine is so we can have a better idea where he may be at any given time."

"Sounds like a plan. Let's do it. How far is it from here?"

He drove back the way they had come. "It's out of town about fifteen miles. Should take about—What ho? Wonder what this is?"

"What?" Margot asked as the sound of a siren behind them interrupted their conversation. She turned in her seat to glance through the back window of the car. "Police. Wonder what they want? You weren't speeding or anything."

"I don't know but he's pegged me for something. I better pull over." Mitch moved the car over to the side of the road and rolled his window down. "Dig in the glove compartment and grab the registration and proof of insurance."

Margot tugged the latch open and, as she shuffled the junk around trying to find the papers, she heard the policeman at the window say, "Driver's license, please."

Mitch handed over his license. "What's the reason for the stop?"

"Seems someone in the neighborhood over there thinks you may be casing the place to rob it. There was a call to the station that the same car has been seen in the area for a couple of days, driving slowly along the street—the same street, mind you—then turning around and going back the way it came. The person who called even got a tag number. Interestingly, that number matches the one on this automobile. What are you doing down here?"

"Good grief. The wife and I are checking out the neighborhood in order to see if we want to buy a place."

"First of all, none are on the market that I can see since there don't appear to be any for sale signs out and, secondly, and I mean this with no offense at all, sir, but with the vehicle you drive, I would bet that you don't have the wherewithal to buy one of these homes since they start at around three-quarters of a million dollars."

Margot raised her eyebrows. "With no yards?"

"You haven't answered my question. Why are you down here?"

"I *did* answer. My wife and I are looking for a place to buy." Mitch reached for his license from the officer.

"I'm going to ask you to step out of the car, sir," the officer said as he pulled the license out of Mitch's reach and wrote something on his pad.

"I'll get out but I didn't do anything illegal, and I can tell you right now that you're going to have a fight on your hands. My wife is a medical doctor and she can afford any house out here." Mitch opened the door to step out.

The officer handed Mitch back his license. "I have your information now, sir. You can go but please stay out of this area unless you're accompanied by a realtor. I don't want to run you in, since I don't have any probable cause, but I *am* keeping a note of your information in case another call comes in." The officer tipped his hat slightly toward Margot. "Ma'am." He nodded and moved toward his patrol car.

As soon as the officer was in his vehicle, Mitch closed his door and placed his hands on the steering wheel.

"Why did you tell that cop I'm a doctor?"

"You are, aren't you? I was thinking fast about why we might be in the area and at least that part was the truth—you know, in case he asked for your ID and checked you out.”

Margot crossed her arms across her chest. “But I'm not a doctor right now.”

“You haven't been defrocked or disbarred or whatever they call that with doctors, have you?”

“It's called suspended or revoked license and, no, I haven't been in trouble like that.”

“I don't understand why you're so reluctant to talk about your time as a doctor and why you aren't working as one. Medical school is expensive and you don't even use your training.”

“It's not relevant to what we're trying to do so drop it, okay? Let's go on and check out where Paul is working so we can get a bead on his schedule as you suggested.”

She wished Mitch would drop the subject. She didn't want to talk about her former career nor be reminded of it at all. She didn't have any doubt that Mitch would eventually ferret out the truth about her retirement from medicine since he was such a good investigator but he needed to back off at the moment.

Mitch glanced over and winked at her. “You *do* know that I won't be happy until I know all of your secrets, right?”

“That's what I'm afraid of.” She smiled, as if to make a joke, but she really *was* scared.

CHAPTER 3

"A liar begins with making a falsehood appear like truth, and ends with making truth itself appear like falsehood." ~ *William Shenstone, English poet (1714-1763)*

Richard walked in the back door of his Craftsman-style house and placed the two bags of groceries on the counter in the kitchen. He called out, "I'm home. I brought some salad fixings and that balsamic dressing you like."

His roommate rolled into the room in his wheelchair. "Thanks for picking that up but I already ordered pizza. It should be here any moment."

"All the more reason to have salad first. What goes better with pizza than salad?"

"I don't know, Rick, maybe a beer or two?" Philip

moved over to the refrigerator, opened the door, and pulled out a craft beer that Richard and his friend had made. Philip twisted the cap off and guzzled about half the liquid in the bottle before placing it on the counter. "Man, that's good. At least your beer is one thing I can still enjoy in this life."

"There's a lot more things to enjoy, you know. If you'd let yourself."

"Don't start on me, man, or I'll reconsider this move back in with you."

"Don't get all bent." Richard reached up into the cabinet and pulled down a bowl to toss the salad in. "I wasn't sure whether to tell you something but decided that you needed to know."

"What?"

"I ran into Janette. She—"

"Stop right there." Philip held his hand up. "I don't want to know. I can't deal with her and I don't want to hear that she misses me and wants to see me. I am *not* going to even entertain that idea. I won't see her."

"Okay. Settle down. I wasn't going to force it, I merely wanted to tell you I saw her in case you heard it from someone else and thought I was keeping secrets from you."

"Who else would I hear it from? You seem to forget that I'm here all day by myself. It's not like I have this grand social or work life."

Richard rinsed the lettuce then tore it in shreds into the

bowl. "You *could* go back to work, you know. The chief offered you that desk job."

Finishing off the last swallow of his beer, Philip said, "I can't do that. It would throw me into contact with Janette every day. You may think I'm an idiot to end the relationship, and sometimes I may even agree with you, but I know it would ultimately not work out. Janette would be with me today if I agreed to it but eventually, she would resent me. I know that as well as I know that I cannot see her every day at work and not want her and what we lost that day I was shot. Don't you think I'd be with her if I could?"

"I don't think she would resent you. She loves you, Phil."

"She loves what we *were*. Not what I *am*. It's a big difference."

The doorbell rang.

"That's the pizza. I ordered enough for us both." Philip rolled toward the front of the house.

Richard shook his head as he broke the snap peas into pieces to add to the salad. He could see both sides of the argument that Philip put forth and didn't have any idea how he himself would react if he were the one who was paralyzed, but he sure hated to see one of his best pals miserable and unhappy.

Couldn't having a loving companion help ease the man's misery?

Philip placed the two boxes on the table. "Pizza's here."

"Grab the plates and let's eat." Richard moved to the table with the salad bowl, tongs, and the bottle of dressing.

After each had served themselves a helping of greens and a slice, Richard said, "I think we should have a welcome back keg party."

"Really? Have you lost your mind? We're grownups now, in case you haven't heard. Not only that, we can't encourage people to come over to our place and drink and risk a DUI. We're cops, remember?"

"Bingo." Richard pointed his folded over piece of pizza at Philip. "You can't deny it. You're a cop, like it or not."

Philip slammed his fork on the table. "That was *not* cool, man."

"It's time you faced it. You were meant to work in law enforcement. Sure, you could draw a disability check but you're bright and hardworking. I predict you'd be bored in no time if you sat home every day. Hell, I bet you already *are* bored, nearly to a comatose state. Why don't you come to work with me tomorrow and at least give it a try?"

"You're never going to let up on me if I don't, are you?"

"No. I'm not." Richard didn't want to get into the discussion, but there was no way he could let it go since it was Richard's fault Philip was in that chair in the first place. The fact that Philip wouldn't allow the love of his life to be in his world was bad enough, but if he gave up his life's goal of working in law enforcement as well, it would kill Richard's soul. Even more dead than it already seemed to be.

"How about this then? I show up tomorrow and, if I hate it, I get to come home and you leave me alone about this subject forever?"

Richard grinned. He knew the man was going to be thrilled to be of use again. "And if you love it?"

"I don't think that'll happen but if it does, I'll take the job and—"

"And thank me every day?"

Philip laughed. "Something like that."

"I'll take that deal." Richard bit into a second piece of pizza. "By the way, is your uniform pressed? If you're going to work tomorrow, you'll need it ironed."

Philip grabbed his second slice from one of the delivery boxes. "Let's just say I'm going in plainclothes tomorrow. Don't press your luck, Higgins."

"Never." Secretly elated that his friend was going to at least try to get some kind of life back, Richard could barely finish eating. He really wanted to shout his joy to the neighborhood. Maybe this first step would lead to more and would eventually ease Richard's own guilt.

જ∾જ

The next morning, Margot ran on the beach and half expected to see Detective Higgins on the lounge chair again. Surprised at the drop her heart took as she realized he wasn't waiting there for her, she trotted across the sand and up to the patio of the hotel. She sat for a few moments to catch her breath. It really was hard to run across the fine, white sand. Her calf muscles ached.

A young couple came out and sat at the table next to the one next to Margot. They appeared to be arguing and didn't seem to care that there was someone there who may overhear them. Margot debated moving away but, by golly, they came out and sat by her so why should she be the one to move?

In a few moments, she was glad she didn't change seats as, strange as it seemed to her, they were bickering about a woman named Patricia Fielding-Murdock. The woman was apparently a realtor who was supposed to meet them at a house they wanted to look at the day before but she ended up not coming to the appointment. Instead, the realtor called the husband later in the day and asked him to come to the house alone. The wife appeared to believe that something went on with the husband and the realtor as she was raving about how long he'd been gone.

It was all Margot could do, at that point, not to lean forward and openly gawk at the couple. How could it be that they were talking about Paul's latest wife? Or could there be two women with the same name in this town?

How did Mitch not know she was a realtor? And was there trouble in the marriage already?

The conversation between the man and woman went on. Margot could sense the man was lying to his wife but how could it be that Paul's wife would already be so disillusioned with the marriage that she would be having affairs with random men she encountered in their search for real estate? It couldn't be true. She must be misunderstanding what was going on. Like the wife obviously was as well.

The man glanced over at Margot and turned to his wife. "We better go. There are a few other places I want to check out. We'll call another realtor if you don't like the one from yesterday."

The wife shoved her chair back and stood. "*Like* her? I never met her and I think she's a husband-stealing witch. Of course, we're going to hire another one."

"She didn't steal your husband. I'm right here." He rose as well and, with his hand on her elbow, led the woman back inside.

Margot sat there a few more minutes, still stunned at the odds that these people would come out where she was and argue about someone she was interested in talking to about some things. It really was a small world after all, wasn't it? She decided right then to find what office Mrs. Fielding-Murdock worked at and call for an appointment. Mitch told that cop yesterday they were looking for a house to buy and so she would pretend to do exactly that.

She headed to her room to change for the day and to make a call to that realtor. As soon as Margot unlocked the door and was inside, she moved straight to the table between the beds and opened the drawer. She pulled out the phone book and flipped quickly to the yellow pages under R. She had to scan several big brokerage ads with lists of the realtors on them before she found the name she sought.

Margot snatched the receiver off the hook and dialed the number. When a woman answered, Margot said, "My name is Margot Jenkins. I'm looking for a house in the downtown Pensacola area and was given Mrs. Fielding-Murdock's name as a good person to help me find the perfect place. Is she available today? I'm only in town for a few days."

"I'll call her on her cell phone. Will you give me a number where she can reach you?"

Margot gave her the number and hung up. She fretted for a moment about giving her real name but decided it probably didn't matter since chances were, Paul had never told his current wife about his former sister-in-law. At least she hoped so.

The return call came as Margot was putting on her make-up. She arranged to meet the realtor at the grocery store parking lot closest to the bay bridge to leave her car and travel to the various houses together. Margot indicated she was only interested in houses with little to no yard to maintain but with high-end appliances and other features. She really wanted to get into some of those houses in the Aragon subdivision. Almost giddy with the anticipation of actually talking to wife number three, Margot slid into a recently purchased pair of shoes, grabbed her purse, and left the room.

Calling Mitch on her way, Margot drove to the grocery store. She wanted to make sure someone knew where she was, but she also wanted to find out why Mitch hadn't found out the line of work Paul's wife was in. He hemmed and hawed around it for a while but Margot finally figured out that Mitch hadn't even tried to find out what the woman did. He presumed she was a housewife. Margot was a bit miffed about that since this was the way to get a chance to chat with the woman and, if she'd known sooner, she could be way ahead of where she found herself now.

A black Volvo whipped in to the parking space next to Margot and, a trim, neatly dressed woman stepped out. The woman tapped on Margot's window. "Are you Miss Jenkins?"

Margot let her window down before answering the question she'd understood from lip reading. "I am. You must be Mrs. Fielding-Murdock."

"Call me Patricia."

"I'm Margot."

The lady took a step back to allow Margot to exit her car. Margot assessed her. She had a similar look and body style to Geneva. Margot bet they could pass for each other in dim light. It was a bit eerie to think the man was seeking out and marrying women who were almost twins to her sister. The second wife also had a more than passing resemblance to Geneva.

"I want to show you some absolutely divine houses first. They're a little pricey but you did say you had an $800,000.00 budget, right? These are worth the money as they're close to everything downtown. The city has a lot of events that go on in the historical area and this is absolutely the best place to live."

"It almost sound like you reside there yourself," Margot said.

"I do. I've lived in Pensacola for years. My family was one of the founding Spanish families. I've only been in Aragon for a year or so now, though. I moved in there when I married."

"Nice. I guess your husband is successful as well."

"Oh, yes. He's got some family money as well as the money he earns from his work." Mrs. Fielding-Murdock pointed to her car. "Come on. I'll take you in to show you the two I think would be perfect for you." She smiled. "You did say you're single, right? This one particular place I think you should see is absolutely wonderful for entertaining—it'll serve you well while dating and throwing bachelorette parties—then, when you do find Mr. Right, it's perfect for the events of marriage. You know, entertaining clients or co-workers as well as throwing an odd baby shower or two."

The woman sure did love to talk. Margot wished the subject of the husband hadn't been so quickly changed. How could she get the woman to keep chatting about her spouse and what he did for a living or around the house? Coming up blank, Margot got in the Volvo and clicked the seat belt into place.

She realized she needed to say something as too much time had passed. "It does sound like the ideal solution. What does the other one you want to show me have that's different?"

"Oh, that one is super in other ways. It has so much architectural detail, it's going to make you swoon—well, I think so—if you're a lover of details, that is."

"I *am* very big fan of details."

"Well, honey, you are going to love this house. It even has a widow's walk."

Pretending to be ignorant, Margot asked, "What's that?"

"You've never seen one?"

"I don't think so."

Margot smiled to herself. This lady was a talker for sure. She seemed very friendly and warm. Margot immediately wanted to protect her. The woman didn't deserve to be another victim of Paul Murdock.

"It's a feature at the top of the house. They're on houses at the shore and are walkways with rails. It's for the wife to look out to sea and wait for her seaman husband to come home. Sadly for a lot of them, their men never returned and the walkways became known as widow's walks."

"That *is* sad. Do these houses overlook the water?" Margot knew they didn't but she didn't want this woman to know she'd already scoped out her own house.

"No. They don't. They're close to the bay front but they don't actually sit on the water." She pointed. "Here we are now. One more turn and we'll be at the first house I was telling you about."

"I can't wait. I love checking out new places. I hope one of them is waiting for me to move right in."

"Me, too, hon. There's nothing I love better than introducing someone to their new home." Patricia put the car in park and smiled over at her passenger. "Here goes."

They each stepped out of their side of the vehicle and made their way across the grass to the front door. Margot glanced around the area and realized the house she was being shown was one street over and three houses down from Murdock's. She couldn't see the driveway, though, to see if the other black Volvo was parked there.

Patricia unlocked the glass-paned front door as Margot scoured her brain for something to say to get the woman to talk about her husband. She had no idea how to broach the subject with Patricia but she really was dying to chat the realtor up about Paul. It was all she could do merely to pay attention to the tour of the house.

They strolled through the downstairs. Margot made all

the noises of approval she could think of while Patricia showed her the six-burner gas chef's oven and the sub-zero refrigerator. The granite countertops were impressive but this was getting Margot nowhere in her investigation.

"Ready to see the upstairs? There are three bedrooms up there. One has an attached bathroom and the other two share a Jack and Jill bathroom."

Patricia's perkiness was starting to rub Margot the wrong way.

"You know what? I feel a horrible headache coming on. I think it's my sinuses. The humidity here seems so oppressive."

"Oh, I completely understand. Do you want to re-schedule?"

Sensing an opportunity, Margot said, "I think I'd be all right if I had something to take, like a sinus pill. Is there a pharmacy nearby where we could go and I could pop in and buy something? I think even some of the convenience stores have small packets of them. I just need to take one and I'm sure I'll be fine."

"I've got good news. I live right down the street. We always have something in the medicine cabinet. Come on. I'll take you to my place and we'll make you better."

Margot hid her glee at getting a chance to check out Paul's house. She walked slowly and as if she were in pain so Patricia would believe she was really ill. Her heart was doing a pitter-patter at the risk she was taking.

If Paul Murdock was home, it was all over. She didn't know what he'd do if he saw her but she was sure it wouldn't be a brotherly hug of recognition.

"Come to the car. It's a short drive and we could actually walk but it'd be better to ride since you feel so bad."

"I'm okay with walking." It dawned on Margot that she didn't have a way back to that grocery store where her car was if Paul was around. Reconsidering her rash plan to get into the house, she glanced over at Patricia. "You know what? I think I'm going to be okay. I feel better already. Maybe it was something inside the house affecting me."

"Oh, I hope not. The builders here were so careful to use materials that would be anti-allergen. It would be a shame to be allergic to such a lovely house. Do you want to try to go back in?"

"I think we should call it a day. Maybe we can try again tomorrow."

"You really do still feel bad, don't you? Come on. I'm taking you to my house. You can take a tablet and have some water. I have a nice sofa you can lie on for a while if you need to."

"I don't want to disturb your family."

"No one is home. My husband and I don't have any children. He doesn't even want a dog, can you imagine?" Tears pooled in Patricia's eyes.

Margot wanted to hug the lady. If Paul didn't even want to let the woman have a pet, what kind of marriage could they have? Margot suspected it wasn't a good one but she was still sorry for Patricia. The perky, happy woman seemed to be headed for doom and disaster. Margot wanted to keep her safe and not allow her to be yet another victim of the awful Paul. "All right. I *could* use some water."

They got in the Volvo and drove around the corner. Margo's gut knotted again as she noticed the other black car in the driveway. "I thought you said no one was home? Whose car is that?"

"It's my husband's but he's gone. He rented a car since his was in the shop. My cousin owns the repair place and he had a couple of his guys bring it back when they got it fixed. Don't worry, even if Paul were here, he wouldn't mind you resting for a while."

"I really hate to be a bother."

"Come on. It's no trouble." Patricia got out of the car and led Margot to the door.

Inside, they went to the kitchen. Patricia pulled a glass out of the cabinet and filled it with water from the filtered faucet. She slid open what Margot would have thought was a roll-top built in breadbox but what really was a lazy Susan. It served as a makeshift medicine cabinet. Patricia spun the device and took a box of tablets from it when they arrived at hand. She turned to look at Margot. "Pretty nifty, huh? It was my husband's idea."

"It *is* clever."

Margot took the box and popped out two pills. She

took them and chased them down with the water.

"I'm going to make a few phone calls. Have a seat in the living room and put your head back on a pillow for a little while. I'll check in on you." Patricia pointed to the way they'd come and added, "I'm going to be right in here at the kitchen bar. Go on and get some shut eye."

Margot walked into the living room and sat. She took her time scoping out the layout and the furniture. The room was opulently furnished with white leather sofas. The end tables and coffee tables were of a bronze metal and there were some pieces of art on the wall made of metal as well. One was surrounded by ornate scrollwork. The room was a little too stark for her taste but she recalled Paul's taste did run to the modern end of the spectrum. Her sister used to bemoan the fact that her husband didn't like her antique quilts and hardwood furniture she'd inherited from their grandmother.

Curious to see if any of the knick-knacks or other items had survived from the time of her sister's marriage to Murdock, Margot peered at the various items on the mantel and side tables. Her heart hammered again at the thought of him catching her in his house but here she was and she intended to at least check out the part of the house she was allowed to see.

As Margo glanced around, she noticed toward the rear of the room, in a dark corner, a spiral wooden staircase. A very similar one to the one her sister died on. She half-rose from her chair as if compelled to investigate the area. Before she could take a step, Margot heard a door slam shut from the direction of the kitchen and a male voice called out.

CHAPTER 4

"Anger is never without a reason,
but seldom with a good one."
Benjamin Franklin, American founding father,
poet and statesman (1705-1790)

Richard couldn't believe his eyes. What in the hell was that woman doing here at the Murdock house? He'd been at the station going over the notes he'd made and decided to take a ride by the residence where the man had moved when he left New Orleans. Stunned to see Margot walking to the door with a woman, Richard resisted the urge to slam on the brakes, but just barely. He didn't have any idea who the other woman was but as he passed the house, he saw her pause by the door then open it.

"Good God. That Jenkins woman really *is* loony tunes.

Why in the world would she reveal herself now?"

He drove on, puzzled about what Margot could be up to. He made it to the end of the street before he decided he had to do something. Turning around, he headed toward the Murdock driveway. There were two cars parked there. Richard hesitated a moment before he got out. What if both the husband and wife were home? This was so not good. Margot said Murdock was dangerous and Richard was inclined to believe her, based on what he'd learned so far. He wasn't sure what he'd find inside if the man was home but he had to believe the guy was smart enough not to hurt her in broad daylight with his wife in the house.

Moving down the driveway and to the door he'd seen the women enter, Richard thought about what he was going to say when he knocked. Having no idea what crazy Margot said to get in the house, he didn't have a clue what kind of story to tell. He knocked and no one answered.

Taking a chance and more than a little worried when no one responded, he pushed on the window in the top of the door. The door opened and he stepped into the kitchen. A gust of wind slammed the door behind him. Startled, Richard called out, "Anyone home?"

The woman who let Margot in the house came through a door at the end of the kitchen. In one hand she carried a teapot and in the other a box of what he presumed were tea bags. She made eye contact with him and jumped back. "What do you want? I don't have any cash here."

"Sorry, sorry. I'm not a criminal. I knocked and no one answered—"

"So you decided to come in, then?"

"No. The door opened and—"

"And, again, you came in?"

"Well, yeah, I guess I did." Sheepish at being caught, Richard tried to put on his best smile. The one Philip said the women swooned over. "I really *am* sorry."

"What do you want? Why'd you knock on my door in the first place?" The woman set the teapot and bags on the counter beside her.

Thinking fast, he said, "I needed to see if I could borrow your phone. My cell died and—"

"Sure. Go ahead. I was making some calls on my own mobile phone but you can use the one on the wall over there." She pointed beside the door.

Richard stepped over to the phone and dialed his phone that was in the car. Thank God he didn't have it in his pocket.

He had a conversation with his phone about his car being broken down, all the while wondering what happened to Margot. How was he going to broach the subject of having seen the other woman without this lady calling the cops? He almost lost his train of thought in the fake conversation as he contemplated his colleagues showing up to arrest him as a burglar.

"Okay, then, I'll try that. Thanks." He replaced the receiver and turned to the woman who stood staring at him. "Looks like I may have some junk in my carburetor. I should be able to clear it quickly if that's the problem. I was able to ease my car into your yard area. It won't be a problem for your husband if I take a few minutes out there, will it?"

"Shouldn't be. He's not home."

Good. One question answered. Now, how could he ask the other—about Margot being there?

"Before you think you're here alone with a helpless woman, I have to tell you, I have a friend in the other room who is probably listening to this conversation with her hand on the number to the police. I also have a gun in this drawer here right beside me." The woman, who Richard now assumed was Mrs. Murdock, tapped the handle to the drawer.

"No worries, ma'am. I'm going." Now that he knew Margot was in the house and safe, he was good to go. He backed into the door and turned the knob behind him. He didn't take his eyes off the woman in case she decided to pull out and use that firearm.

When Richard was in the driveway, he jogged down the slope to his car and popped the hood. He pretended to fiddle with the engine for a while in case Murdock's wife was watching from the window. He idly wondered why Margot hadn't come into the kitchen and hoped she truly was in shape to move about and that Mrs. Murdock hadn't lied about Mr. Murdock being there.

Concerned now that maybe she was lying, Richard almost went back up to the house but before he could make a move, Mrs. Murdock came out onto her front porch and called out, "Sir?"

He lifted his head then turned to face her. "Yes?"

"My friend seems to have left. Did you see a brown-haired woman come by while you were here?"

"No. I haven't seen a soul. This is a quiet neighborhood."

Mrs. Murdock walked across her grass and over to where he stood. "It's odd. Her car is over at the grocery store in Gulf Breeze and I was going to take her back to it but she seems to have left. I can't figure it out. We went inside so she could take a sinus pill and now she's gone. Strange."

"It's too dangerous for her to walk across the three mile bridge. I wonder why she would leave like that?" Now Richard was worried. Was he going to have to get a warrant to go in after her? He'd seen Margot enter the house and didn't see her exit. What the heck was this all about? Was Mrs. Murdock being concerned about her "friend" an act?

"I don't know how she's going to get back there. I guess she called a cab while we were talking. It's too bad though because I really wanted to sell her a house."

Richard shook his head. "Sell her a house?"

"Yeah. I'm a realtor and she fell ill in one of the places I was showing her. I brought her to my place since I live so close and gave her a couple of sinus pills. I hope she'll call me again because I could tell she had the money to buy what I wanted to show her and I could sure use the commission."

Ready now to be gone and see if he could catch up to Margot at the grocery store, Richard said, "Let me see if this thing will crank now so I can get out of your way." He moved to the driver's side, opened the door and turned the key. Of course it started.

He walked back to the front of the vehicle and slammed the hood closed. "Thanks again for the use of your phone."

"You're welcome." Mrs. Murdock sauntered toward her front door.

He got in his car and drove away, glancing at each side of the road as he went, searching for Margot. He still wasn't quite sure what was going on and if she was still in the Murdock house in danger or not.

❦

At Veteran's Memorial Park, Margot sat on one of the benches and stared at the Vietnam memorial which was a half replica of the Wall in Washington DC and was called the Wall South. She thanked her stars that she'd been able to sneak out of Paul Murdock's house before he saw her. Man, when she heard the male voice from the kitchen, her heart stopped. She couldn't catch her breath for a few moments and, when she finally could, she eased out of the living room. She stealthily opened the door that led to the front porch and shut it behind her with a soft click.

Once out of the house, she noticed a nondescript sedan parked near the curb but didn't stop to figure out who it might belong to since she presumed it belonged to whomever Murdock got to bring him home since his car had been in the shop.

Cursing the uncomfortable shoes she had on, Margot jogged down the street until she reached the main road. She moved down it pretty quickly even though she could feel the blisters forming. Fretting about how to get across the bay bridge without getting killed, she saw the park and decided to find a seat there and call Mitch to come get her.

Lord, he was probably going to kill her for doing such a stupid thing as going to Murdock's house. She'd known it was dumb when she did it and she certainly didn't relish a lecture but she saw no way to get out of it.

Margot pulled off one shoe and rubbed her instep. Dreading putting the shoe back on, she took off the other one and rubbed the bottom of her feet on the concrete. The roughness of the surface actually felt pretty good on her poor soles. It was nice to be outside in the warm air. She enjoyed it for a while and about the time she decided to make that call to Mitch, a car pulled in to the parking area.

Richard Higgins stepped out of the driver's side of the

vehicle and stalked over to where she sat. Before he could open his mouth, she said, "How did you find me?"

"Are you nuts?" he asked then held up his hand as she opened her mouth, "no, wait. Don't answer that. Of course, you are."

"What the hell is your deal? You can't talk to me like that." She stood. The concrete pebbles poked her in the feet. It wasn't as comfortable standing on it as running her aching arches across it.

"I can and I will. What were you thinking to go into Murdock's house like that? You could have been killed." Richard grabbed her in a kind of hug. Not really a hug, more like an *I'm grateful you didn't die on my watch* embrace—one that hurt—a lot.

"Let me go. I'm fine."

He released her.

She spun her arms in the air. "See. I'm in one piece. Nothing happened." She stopped. "Wait one second. Did you *follow* me?"

"No. I didn't. I was—"

"You were *what,* exactly?"

"Good Lord, I've been interrupted all day by women. I swear, I'm going to quit talking to anyone of the female persuasion."

"Tell me how you know I was in Paul Murdock's house. You tell me right now." She was out of control angry and couldn't figure out why. If Paul had been home and the cop was following her, it would've been a good thing as the detective would've been ready to enter the house to help her. She couldn't believe she was so mad but there it was.

"I saw you go in. I was doing a drive-by, and imagine my surprise to see you strolling along with some unknown woman and then you entered that house. I couldn't believe it."

Margot sat on the bench with a thud. "I was trying to establish a relationship with her. I found out she's a realtor so I made up that I was looking for a house to buy. Let's just say I borrowed a cover story from a pal because I needed to make friends with her so I can tell her to run from Paul before she gets killed."

"I have no idea what you mean about borrowing a cover story but I do know when I saw Paul Murdock's car in the driveway, I almost panicked because I thought he would harm you if he saw you, and so I went in the kitchen door."

"Oh, God. That was you?"

"Huh? What do you mean?"

"I was in the living room after faking a headache and I heard the kitchen door slam shut. The male voice calling out scared me—I thought it might be Paul—and I took off out the front door."

She shook her head. Unreal. She'd fled and looked like an idiot now to Patricia Murdock, and all because of Richard going in the back door.

"That explains it then."

"Explains what?"

"Why Mrs. Murdock was so befuddled that you were gone."

"So now I appear to her to be some kind of flake because of you."

"Oh, no, you can't put that on me, lady. You've made your own crazy world and everyone who meets you somehow gets dragged into it." He stood. "Now, I'm willing to give you a ride to your car so you don't get killed. Do you want to come with me?"

"I don't know if I should since you called me crazy—" She paused for two beats. "Twice."

Richard laughed. "You *are* crazy. You may as well own it, baby."

She didn't disagree this time, since she really couldn't because he was right. She'd acted in a totally irresponsible way and could have easily died if Paul Murdock had really been home.

A bit chagrined, she stood. "Okay. Take me to my car. I won't argue the crazy for now."

"Glad to hear you can be reasonable." Richard held out his hand. "I see your poor feet are red and swollen. Want me to carry you to my car?"

"Very funny. No." She stepped onto the grass and walked across it even though it had a sign to keep off.

"Do I have to arrest you?" he called out behind her.

"I'm killing the grass? Is that considered homicide?"

"I have arrest powers for other things as well, my dear

lady, not merely homicide."

She kept walking until she got to his car then stood and tapped her foot until he got there from taking the long way round—the legal way around.

Richard stepped over to the passenger side and unlocked Margot's door. "Hop in and I'll take you to your car. It's in the parking lot of the grocery store across the bridge, right?"

"Yeah. I parked near the chicken restaurant." She opened the door and tossed her shoes inside before she climbed in herself.

Once Richard was seated on the driver's side, he nodded at the floorboard. "Why do you women do that to yourselves?"

"Do what?"

"Wear shoes that clearly are too tight or too uncomfortable for long-time wear. It seems to be some kind of punishment you ladies have to do to atone for your sins."

"If wearing pretty shoes is atonement for sin, I must have really offended someone recently since this pair is actually hell on earth." She laughed. "I can't figure it out. They were fine in the store."

He turned the key to crank the engine.

"Not so fine to be making a getaway from a possibly homicidal former brother-in-law, are they?"

"Now that you mention it, yeah."

"By the way, what color are we calling those? I don't think I've ever seen a pair in such an odd shade." Richard indicated the shoes with a tilt of his head.

"Do you have a shoe fetish or something?"

"No. Why?"

"You seem to pay a lot of attention to them for someone of the male species."

"Let's just say I've been with a lot of ladies who have suffered with ill-fitting shoes and I've learned to be leery of a high heel."

"Why is that?" She couldn't help but giggle at his tone of voice. He sounded as if he had paid some kind of high price at one time as a result of someone's shoe choice.

"Let's leave it at my former wife was notorious for buying shoes that were too small for her and call it a day, okay?"

"Someday you'll have to tell me that story." Margot grinned, curious about both his former wife and her taste in shoes. "By the way, the shoes are lemon yellow. Or at least that's what was printed on the box."

Richard shook his head, muttered, "Lemon yellow, good grief," under his breath, and eased out of the parking space. He made his way around to the exit and out into the street traffic.

When they arrived at the location of Margot's car, he pulled in beside it and turned to look at her. "I hope we'll have those files the chief requested by tomorrow afternoon. Do you think you can stay out of trouble for the morning and meet me at the station around three?"

"I kind of resent you for thinking I was in trouble back

there. I'm a grown woman and I can take care of myself."

"Listen, I get that you're an adult and responsible for your own actions but you really put yourself in a potential mess when you went in that house with Murdock's wife. What if he'd been there or come home while you were lounging around his living room with a fake headache? You could very well have been his next victim—in fact, I thought you were when I didn't see—"

"You were worried about me?"

"I saw you go in, I noticed Murdock's car in the driveway, and when I went in, I didn't see you anywhere. I was almost to the point of identifying myself as an officer and searching the house for you."

"Wow. I had no idea."

"Of course, you didn't. That's my point. You think you know what you're doing—either that, or no offense—you're too arrogant to consider the rashness of your actions—"

"Arrogant? Rash?"

"Yes, rash for sure. You find out Murdock's wife's a realtor and off you go on a tear to get her to show you houses so you can get to know her and maybe get inside her head or her house, never thinking about the consequences or the potential risk to your own safety."

"I was careful. I saw his car in the driveway and found out he wasn't home before I went inside with her."

"But he could've come home at any time. Did you spend one minute thinking about what you'd do or say if he walked in and said, 'Hello, dear sister-in-law'?" Richard leaned toward Margot. His face almost in hers, he added, "Did you?"

Taken aback at his tone of voice, she recoiled and almost whacked her head on the window. "I can't say that I really did."

Richard straightened up. "See what I mean about staying out of trouble? Can you promise me that you won't pull any more bone-headed stunts?"

She opened her door. "I *will* say that I won't return to the Murdock house without letting you know ahead of time, but I can't make a promise that I may not be able to keep." Margot stepped out of the car then leaned in so she could see Richard's eyes. "I appreciate the ride and I'll see you tomorrow at three." She slammed the door and, strolling around the back of Richard's car, she made her way to her own vehicle.

Once inside, she backed out of the parking spot and drove away toward the beach, never glancing in the rearview mirror to see if he followed her.

CHAPTER 5

"Keep love in your heart. A life without it is like a sun-
less garden when the flowers are dead."
Oscar Wilde, Irish writer and poet (1854-1900)

That evening, Richard and Philip decided to take a drive to one of Philip's favorite places to eat since he'd not been since he got out of rehab.

Arriving at Sam's Seafood on Main Street, Philip parked the handicapped-equipped van his insurance company had provided for him after his on-the-job injury. Richard was impressed with how well his roommate coped with the hand controls. The man was already driving the thing as if he'd only ever driven without his legs.

They exited the automobile and made their way inside the restaurant. Seated at one of the tables near the side door, they perused the menu even though they both already knew what they would be ordering. Richard's favorite item on the menu was the fried shrimp and oyster combo and Philip always ordered a bowl of gumbo and the grouper. Before the waitress came to bring the drinks they ordered as she seated them, Philip said, "Another thing to hate about this wheelchair is we can't sit in one of the tall-backed booths and be kind of anonymous. This table seating puts us right out in the middle of the room."

"You hiding out from someone?"

"I might be. You never know who might come in."

"These menus are big enough to hide behind. If someone you don't want to speak to comes in, open it and no one will see you." Richard illustrated what he meant by opening his and ducking his head down.

"They'd still see my hardware so it wouldn't matter about hiding my face."

The bitterness in Philip's voice reminded Richard that his friend still had a long way to go before he accepted the way his life had changed. Shame at his own role in his roommate's new circumstances roiled in his stomach and almost made him vomit.

Desperate to change the subject, Richard glanced around the room. He noticed someone they both knew and nodded in the woman's direction.

"Look, there's Regina from Judge Jacobs's office. Don't you know her from the warrants run?"

"Yeah. I haven't seen her in a while." Philip turned his head toward where Richard had indicated. "Who's she with? Should we invite them to join us?"

"Oh, crap. No. Man, oh, man, I'm sorry."

"What? What is it?" Philip asked.

"I had no idea she'd be here. I can't believe it."

"*What?*"

"It's Janette."

Philip's eyes got large. He put his hands on the wheels of his chair and made a move backward. "Why did you bring me here? To try to get us back together? You need to stop. Let it go."

"No, *you* need to stop. You're the one who suggested this place. I had nothing to do with it. I didn't tell her we were going to be here and she certainly didn't follow us. If you would take a second to pay attention, you'll see she's almost done with her food. If anything, she could accuse us of coming here because we knew she was here. Neither of us had any idea, but she could presume we did, couldn't she?"

Philip let go of his wheels and placed his hands on the table. His knuckles clenched into fists but he did stay. "You're right. I need to get a grip. If I'm going to live in the same town as Janette, I have to expect to run into her sooner or later. I have to learn to deal with it."

"And if you take the job at the station, you'll definitely run into her, so it may be good to get that first awkward meeting over with sooner as opposed to later."

"Easy for you to say. It's not going to rip your heart right out of your chest."

The waitress brought their drinks and took their orders. As soon as she was gone, Richard picked up the conversation where it left off. "If your heart is still that deeply invested in Janette, why break it off?"

"Because I'm half a man." Tears welled in Philip's eyes but didn't escape. Richard could tell it was taking all the man had in him not to break down and wished he hadn't pushed him by asking the question.

"You're *not* half a man but this isn't the place to get into that conversation and I'm sorry I asked since it's clearly a sore subject. One day I'll learn to keep my mouth shut." Richard picked up his napkin-wrapped cutlery, slid off the paper ring and unfurled the white napkin.

"I doubt that. You'll never learn to rein in that tongue of yours."

"You're probably right but let's talk about something else besides women and love lives while we wait for our food."

Philip smiled a tiny smile. "Good idea. What's left? Religion, politics?"

"Those are safe subjects for sure."

They both laughed and in a few moments, Janette and Regina passed by the table on their way out the door on the "A" Street side of the restaurant.

Regina spoke first. She placed her hand on Philip's left shoulder. "How are you doing?"

"I'm adjusting. Thanks."

"How long have you been back in town? I heard you

were coming home but wasn't sure when."

Richard could tell Philip was trying his best not to look at Janette but to focus on Regina by keeping his eyes firmly on Regina's face. "I've been back a week or so. Richard was good enough to allow me to return to live at his house and even adjusted his place to meet my needs."

Regina tapped her index finger on Philip's shoulder. "I hope you'll come by the courthouse and visit sometime. The judge was talking about you the other day and wondering how you were getting along."

"Like I said, I'm good. I even went in to the station today for a while and talked to the chief and the guys."

"That's wonderful," Janette said as she stepped from behind Regina. "Does that mean you're going to go back to work?"

Richard noticed Philip's face harden when his former fiancée spoke. He opened his mouth to beat Philip to an answer in case the man was going to be rude but before he could make a sound, Philip responded, "I'm not sure. It was a nice visit but I'm not sold on the job the chief has offered. Thank you for asking."

Janette had started to smile when Philip addressed her but by the time he finished, she looked crestfallen at his icy tone and seeming brushoff.

Regina placed her hand on Janette's upper arm. "Let's go. The waitress is on her way with the food for these two. We should get out of the way."

It seemed to Richard that Regina was practically pushing Janette to the door. "See you ladies later," he said.

He watched them until they were outside then turned to face Philip to compliment him on how he faced Janette without falling apart. Stunned at the expression on his roommate's face, Richard almost choked. His face was so red the man could very well be having some kind of stroke. Richard had never seen him so angry.

The waitress set their food down and scooted away as if to escape the rancor emanating off Philip. Strong emotion emanated from him so solidly, the man fairly vibrated with it.

Philip put his head down and dove into the grouper in a savage manner. He ripped the meat apart using his knife and fork as if he were skinning a rhinoceros. The steam wafted across the table in Richard's direction.

Taking a hint from the way his friend was attacking his food, Richard decided not to say a word while they ate. Philip would talk when he was ready.

Richard reached for the cocktail sauce to put some on his plate to dip his fried oysters and peered through his lashes at Philip. Like a slam to the chest, Richard realized his companion wasn't angry but was trying to hide his heartrending anguish and maybe even a few unshed tears.

℘℘℘

The next morning, after a night spent online looking up other properties she might pretend to want to see and coming up with a plausible story to tell Patricia about why she took off the day before, Margot rose early for another run. She was never a runner when she practiced medicine since she didn't make the time, but once she left the field, she needed the thinking time. She did her best mulling and decision-making when she ran. It had helped her through the rough patches more than once.

She ran for several miles down the beach to the Fort Pickens gate then turned and ran back to the hotel, all the while thinking about her sister. It was paramount that Paul pay for what he'd done to rip their family apart. Her parents went to their deaths believing their daughter died in an accident and for that Margot was grateful. She wouldn't have wanted them to know their son-in-law whom they adored was such a manipulative cold-blooded bastard as to kill their beautiful daughter for money. Margot was fooled by him too and couldn't forgive herself for not realizing her sister was in peril and help her.

Truth be known—and it was this truth that haunted her to this day— Margot had been jealous of her sister all their lives. Geneva was the favorite child. She was golden and blonde. Popular and everything came easy to her. Margot was the one who had to work hard and was almost a nonentity in school. She couldn't recall the number of times that someone would befriend her once they found out she was Geneva's sister so they could get close to Geneva. It hurt too much to dwell on that part of the past.

Her heels thudded on the sand as Margot finished her run. She pushed the old pangs of envy to the back of her mind and squared her shoulders. No matter how wonderful Geneva's life had been, the truth was, she was gone and Margot could only try to make some type of atonement for her lifetime resentment towards her sister. She loved her but she'd always wanted somehow to be her.

Even attending medical school was a decision made to try to show up Geneva. Margot had the brains to complete the tough schedule, the internship, and residency but Geneva was still winning medals swimming while Margot was training to be a medical examiner. Geneva missed her chance at the Olympics when she had to have an emergency appendectomy while at the venue for the race so she got national press attention for that the same week Margot got named as chief resident at her hospital.

When her sister died, Margot was filled with guilt for all of the years of resentment and now that it was quite likely that she was murdered, Margot's guilt was at a fever pitch. She had to act. Paul *had* to pay. Margot would give up her own life to have Geneva alive again.

Margot entered the hotel's door from the gulf side entrance and made her way to her room. Once inside, she noticed the red light flashing on the phone beside the bed. Listening to the message while shoving her running shoes off with her toes at the heels, she grabbed the pen beside the pad in case she needed to write down anything.

"It's Richard Higgins. The files came in early. I'm at

the station in one of the conference rooms. I've left a visitor's pass for you with the desk sergeant. Come when you can. I'm starting without you."

"Blast it. I ran too long. So much for that three o'clock appointment." She tossed the receiver on its cradle and jerked her T-shirt over her head. Walking toward the shower, she peeled off her spandex running pants and almost tripped over her feet in her mad dash to get herself clean and to the police station.

Once dressed in a white linen suit with navy blue shell and navy pumps, Margot drove to the station. She checked in with the desk sergeant and, as she clipped her visitor's pass to her lapel, followed the man to the conference room.

Upon entry, she noticed Richard seated at one end of the table with his jacket off but his shoulder holster still on. The sleeves of his pale blue button-front shirt were rolled up to the elbow exposing strong, veined forearms. Margot almost swooned at the sight. She was such a sucker for a man with a shoulder holster who had the body to pull it off. It seemed to her that such an accessory set off the muscular chest in just the right way. She shook herself.

She was not here to admire this man. She had a job to do and, by God, she needed to get serious about it.

Richard glanced up from the open file in front of him. "Oh, good. You're here. Do you want some coffee or something?"

"Absolutely. That would be divine."

He jerked his thumb over his shoulder. "Over there on the side table. I had them bring in a thermos as well as some cream and sugar. Help yourself."

She moved to the side table and grabbed a paper cup.

"Fair warning. The sergeant made it and it's pretty strong. It could actually take a stroll down the street with you, so if you don't like it that way, I recommend a ton of sugar and a lot of the cream. Kind of disguises the taste."

"I don't mind it strong." Margot poured herself half a cup and deciding it did resemble some kind of sludge or maybe liquid road tar, dumped in some sugar. She took a sip and made a face.

"I tried to tell you."

"You can't even see me. I'm behind you. How could you tell I didn't like it?"

"I heard the way you swallowed."

Margot walked around the back of Richard's chair and took a seat beside him at the table. "What does that even mean?"

"It means you swallowed so hard, you almost gagged. That makes a sound." He indicated the other files on the desk. "Grab one. I'm looking at the New Orleans autopsy file."

Margot reached for the closest file. "You must be the oddest man I've ever met."

"Why's that?"

"You can hear someone swallow from behind and you

picked out my accent the other day. It's almost like magic."

"I'm related to Sherlock Holmes." He winked.

Or at least she thought he did. Surely he didn't.

"You *do* know he's a fictional character, don't you?"

"Interestingly, he's based on a real person. A medical doctor whom Arthur Conan Doyle studied under at Edinburgh University."

"And *that* guy is your relative?" Margot asked.

"No."

"But you said you were related." She opened the file she'd chosen.

"You call *me* odd?" He jotted a note on the legal pad beside the file he was studying.

"What does that mean?"

"It means you're the most literal woman I've ever met. The phrase 'I'm related to him' didn't mean I was truly related. It meant I was comparing my mad skills to his. Nothing more."

"Oh, I get it. I wasn't sure, especially when you started talking about the real doctor the character was based on."

"I see now how you got through medical school. You're—"

"I'm what?"

"Sorry, lady, but it's got to be said."

"What?"

"You're a bit anal, aren't you?"

Shocked at how what he said pierced her heart, Margot ducked her head down and tried to focus on the words that appeared to be swimming in front of her eyes. Determined not to let him see how he'd affected her, she said, "Enough chatter. We're here to work."

"Right. Gotcha." Richard focused on his own file. Out of the corner of her eye, she could see him jot a few more notes.

They each worked silently for a while with Margot only focusing once in a while on Richard's comments about her. She really did try to be less serious on occasion but her personality was such that she couldn't help herself. He was an attractive man and, even though she knew she wasn't gorgeous, she knew she wasn't hideous either. She also acknowledged to herself that he was out of her league. He could have any woman he wanted with his personality and his looks but she knew she would never be his choice as he'd made perfectly clear by his observation about her being anal.

Being anal was a good thing in some ways, wasn't it? She brought her mind back to the case file in front of her. Shocked at how her mind had been wandering into the strange territory while she tried to look at autopsy photos, it dawned on her that she was doing it in an effort to distance herself from the fact that she was staring at her dead sister.

As soon as that thought flitted across her mind, nausea flooded over her. She leapt from the chair, causing it to fall to the floor and bounce a little. She placed her hand over her mouth and ran out into the hallway where she slid down the wall and ended up crouched on the floor.

CHAPTER 6

"The best teamwork comes from men who are working independently toward one goal in unison."
James Cash Penney, American (1875-1971)

Richard sat in shock. He'd noticed Margot was going through the autopsy photos of her sister but since she was a doctor, he sure didn't expect her to lose it when she saw the pictures. Didn't she say she'd been a medical examiner? Did he misunderstand that?

Heaving a large sigh, he pushed away from the table and to his feet. He walked out to the hallway, fully expecting to have to make his way to the ladies' room where he thought his unofficial partner might be heaving her guts out, but she was sitting on the floor right outside the door—in her white slacks, with seemingly no concern at all at them getting dirty on the nasty floor.

He looked down at here and, knowing better but not being able to resist, asked, "Comfy?"

"Very funny, Sherlock."

He held out his hand to assist her to her feet. "Seriously, are you all right? The ladies' room is right down the hall there if you need to freshen yourself. You've probably ruined those slacks."

"I'm fine." Margot took hold of the proffered hand and let him lift her off the tiled floor. "I had a momentary panic as I recalled those weren't only autopsy photos but actually my sister. The girl I shared a room with until the fourth grade. It hit home all of a sudden that this wasn't a standard file review." She smoothed her pants with her hands on her thighs. "Let's get back to it."

"If you're sure."

"I'm sure. I want to get Paul Murdock for these murders, and I can only do it if I separate my emotions from the work I need to tackle."

Richard led the way into the room. "Before you left, did you find anything out of the ordinary?"

"Thanks for resisting the urge to say something worse. I know it was hard not to be sarcastic."

"What?"

Margot followed him into the room and picked up the chair. She sat. "It seems to me that you rely an awful lot on wit and sarcasm in your communications with me. I don't know you well enough to know if this is some coping mechanism in general or if this is something you use to relate to me in particular. Since that appears to be your preferred method of dealing with things, I expected you to have some facetious comment on our way into the room."

"Is this an attempt at a medical diagnosis?"

"Not really." Margot glanced down at the photos she'd run out on. "Let's get back to it."

"Nothing so far?"

"No. Let me keep digging a while longer."

"Fine by me. I've finished with these pictures. I made some notes but when you're done with those there, I'd like to set them all out and compare them side by side."

"Let me look at those first, too before we compare them to each other. Is that okay?"

"Sure. Take your time. I'm going to dive into the case notes from the officer in charge of the New Orleans case. I already made notes on the Reno file while I was waiting for you to arrive." Richard opened the next closest file on the table and dug in.

Periodically, he glanced over at the woman in the other chair. She was close enough that he could see what she was studying but he hoped she couldn't tell he was watching her. She was definitely an enigma, what with her expensive clothes and seriousness but he could also discern a lot of sadness in her. He was dying to know why she wasn't practicing medicine any longer and why she got so upset a few moments prior with the pictures.

Sure, it was her sister but, really, she *had* been a medical examiner. Why would she get queasy? It was a mystery he was committed to solving.

He wondered again why she wasn't working as a doctor and what she could be doing to continue to make the kind of money she had to be pulling down to keep herself in the fancy duds she wore. Yep, the lady was a puzzle.

"Why are you staring at me?"

Margot's abrupt question startled him. He was shocked to find the sound of her voice made him jump in his seat.

"Am I?"

"Yes. You haven't written a word in quite a while and in fact, haven't even turned a page in that file."

"I thought you were paying attention to your own work over there. What are you doing asking me what I'm up to?"

He hoped he could deflect her question by playing dumb, but no such luck.

"Very funny, but I'm not an idiot. You were clearly watching me work and I want to know why."

"I'm interested in your process. Seeing as you have training in this kind of work, I'm curious about what you look for in reviewing one of these reports and autopsy photos. I've been in on post-mortems live with our ME but I was wondering how you make conclusions having not been there in person."

"That sounds like a complete and utter lie to me. If

you wanted to know these things, why not ask?"

"I'm asking now. Will you share your process with me?" Richard smiled the way he'd been told by a former girlfriend was a sure-fire way to win over a woman. He hated to use what she'd called his secret weapon but he sensed he needed it to dig himself out of the hole he'd somehow fallen into without even noticing the downward trajectory.

"I'll even pretend you weren't goofing off if you want me to if you pay attention now and help me get the scumbag that killed my sister."

"If I take a solemn vow to pay close attention from now on?"

"Yes. That's it exactly. You seem to hide behind sarcasm, Detective and someday I hope we can have a conversation without it but for now, I'm afraid I'll have to suck it up and deal with your idiosyncrasy." Margot glanced over at him and smiled. "I'm not usually such a nitpicker but I feel like I need to keep you on task. I can't figure out how you got to be a detective at such a young age when you seem to be all over the place in working this case."

"It may seem to you as if I am moving from one bad idea to another but I really do know what I'm doing. I have a very high rate of case closure. I may go about obtaining results in a way people aren't comfortable with, but I get there."

"Fine, whatever. Come closer and check out what I'm seeing. Look here at this wound on the back of Geneva's head." Margot tapped the photo with the tip of her pen.

Richard leaned over her shoulder to see what she was pointing to. "What?"

"See how there's a gash here? And then another one here and here?" Each time she said the word *here* she tapped the photo again.

"Yeah? What about it?"

Margot shuffled through some of the photos until she stopped on one that showed the wall with blood spatter all over it. She also pulled out one with blood on the actual steps.

"I don't think all these injuries on her head would be caused by a fall. I think she must have been hit with some kind of object." Margot touched the blood on the wall in the second picture. "This appears to be spatter from a hit, not a fall. I can't see how the amount of blood on the sheetrock could possible occur from the allegation that she fell and hit her head. This bigger gash here seems larger than it would be from her falling down. It's more like someone hit her with something and the blood flew outward to mark the wall."

Reaching for the other file, the one of Jill Sikes from New Orleans, Margot shuffled through the photos and pulled out two. "It looks like the same thing happened here. Look."

She tapped the photo of the second Mrs. Murdock's

head then touched the one of the blood on the wall by the staircase in that home.

Richard grabbed all the pictures and flipped through them. "I see what you mean but not being an expert on blood spatter—and I presume you aren't either— how can you tell this isn't the right amount of spatter? How would it have gotten past two investigations? I mean, the two different cases were investigated by two different departments. How would they each miss something like this?"

"I don't know." She shrugged. "Maybe they were too trusting of Paul's statements about his wife's fall both times?"

"Seems weird to me. I know we always take a hard look at any suspicious death—one clearly not based on some medical condition, I mean. I have a tough time believing this man could commit the same crime twice and each of the law enforcement agencies turned a blind eye."

"I agree that it's odd but, clearly, it happened. You can't help but notice the similarities when you place all the photos next to each other." Margot stood. "Watch."

She took several more photos from each of the files and started tossing them on the floor in long lines with her sister's on the top row and the second wife Jill's on the bottom row. Richard shook his head as he paced along beside her. Once she completed the task, they stood side by side and stared down at the pictures.

Astounded at the almost exact nature of the wounds on

both ladies, Richard knelt down beside the photos. He ran his hand over them. "This really *is* crazy. How could the splatter pattern be the same in both? Unless Murdock used the same weapon to kill them both and handled it in exactly the same way, right? Two falls couldn't result in the exact same blood spray. The odds must be astronomical for that to happen."

"I agree. It sure couldn't be an accident."

"No way." Richard shook his head again. "I think I've got to get the chief to contact these other chiefs to coordinate some kind of joint investigation."

"Looks like it to me, too."

Richard stood and crossed his arms. "Would your parents be open to having your sister's body exhumed?"

"Why would that be necessary?"

"Surely you see that it would be. Didn't you say you were a medical examiner?"

She nodded. "I was, yes."

"I have to say, lady, I'm not sure I believe that part of your story."

"What the heck does that mean?"

"Come. Sit." Richard stepped to the table and pulled out a chair for Margot.

She didn't move. "I want to know what you meant by that comment. Are you calling me a liar?"

"It seems weird to me is all."

"What does?"

"This whole story about being a medical examiner

who isn't anymore and a woman who gets nauseated when she looks at autopsy photos seems to be a bit of an untruth."

"Oh, good Lord. There's nothing to that. It's totally different to see a stranger as a corpse than it is to see your own sister on the slab. Why's that so hard to believe?"

"That, in and of itself, makes sense but what about this *used to be a doctor* thing? What do you do now to keep yourself in the style you've clearly become accustomed to?" Richard sat and waved his hand to take in her attire.

"Are you accusing me of something?"

"You have *got* to be the tetchiest woman I've ever met."

Margot crossed her arms. "I am *not* but you've insulted me over and over ever since I met you. You've called me a liar and now you think I'm irritable? You haven't even begun to see me irritated."

"I can't win with you. I give up trying. I'm going to talk to the captain and ask him to give your parents a call. With Murdock being a suspect, we can ask a judge to allow them to be considered the next of kin to allow the exhumation."

"My parents are dead. You have to deal with me as Geneva's only living sibling."

"Well, isn't that just peachy?" Richard said, sarcasm dripping from his voice as he stalked out of the room and down the hall to the chief's office.

托托托

Margot flopped into the pulled-out chair as soon as Richard left the room. She exhaled a deep sigh, so deep it seemed to come from her very soul. She wanted to cry. Why was the man so mean all the time? It was almost as if he had some kind of personal animosity toward her and she couldn't fathom why. She'd been nothing but nice every time she came into contact with him. What good would it do to bring herself to his level of rudeness since she desperately needed his help?

A tiny inner voice niggled at her. Yes, she had been a bit rude to him as well, but it was only because he pushed and pushed until she retaliated. The voice also reminded her she hadn't been forthcoming about herself. Perhaps if she opened up a little and told him why she wasn't practicing medicine, he might understand and be a little more tolerant?

She didn't relish sharing her innermost turmoil with the man but she really wanted him to assist her in making sure Paul Murdock paid for his crimes.

The decision made to open up to the detective, Margot stood and gathered the photos from the floor to replace them into their correct folders. Her gut clenched as she thought about what she'd say to the man about her situation, but she worked diligently to get the files back in order before he returned.

When Richard came back with the chief, Margot was almost finished with her task. She glanced up from her work to catch a look on the detective's face that made her wonder what kind of trouble she was in now. How was it he could make her feel like a naughty little kid every time he came near her? She was a capable adult. Why was he affecting her this way?

"What's wrong, Detective Higgins?" she asked.

"I wanted to show the chief the photos and how they compared and you've packed them away."

"Not a problem. I can get them out again. This time on the table rather than on the floor. How's that?"

"Sounds fine to me, ma'am," the chief said. He stepped around Richard and over to the table. "Let's see what you got."

Margot pulled out the pictures and laid them side by side on the table without saying a word. She decided they should speak for themselves. If what she and Richard had seen was readily apparent to the chief, all the better.

The chief stood, knuckles on the tabletop. After a few moments, he said, "Why didn't someone find this before now?"

"I don't know, sir," Margot said. "Maybe no one looked at them together."

"What I mean is—and it's a rhetorical question at this moment, ma'am—why the hell didn't the New Orleans police department ask for these records when the Murdock man's second wife died? Who screwed this up?" He turned to face Richard. "It seems I have some more calls to make. This man needs to go down and sooner rather than later. Come with me."

"I think we may have enough to ask for a warrant based on these, don't you?" Richard addressed the chief.

"Not yet, but we will as soon as get some more information from the investigating officers. This was some sloppy police work here." The chief nodded at Margot. "You'll excuse us. We have some business to tend to. Grab the files, Detective." He pivoted on his heel and left the room.

"Will you let me know what happens?" Margot asked Richard.

"I'll tell you what the chief says I can. It's the best I can do."

"Can we meet for a drink when you get done? There's something I want to talk to you about."

He ran his hand over his forehead, disturbing the curls that flopped there. "Please tell me there's nothing else you have up your sleeve for me to deal with."

"If I didn't know better, I'd think by your tone of voice that you're making a joke." She couldn't help herself. He looked so cute she had to smile.

"To tell the truth, I actually was."

"Nice to know you have a sense of humor along with the sarcasm."

"That *was* sarcasm, Miss Jenkins." He grinned and patted the back of the closest chair. "I have to go."

"Okay. I know, but when and where for the drink?"

"How about eight tonight at the End of the Alley Bar?"

"Can I find it on my GPS?"

"Yeah. It's easy. It's in Seville Quarter on Government Street, kind of kitty-corner from Plaza Ferdinand."

"I know where that park is. See you there."

Richard grabbed the files as well as the loose photos on the table and left, waving his hand over his head as he went.

As soon as he was gone, Margot pulled out her phone and searched the address of the bar so she could enter it into her GPS.

Once that task was complete, she headed to the desk sergeant's post to return her visitor's pass.

At her car, she called Mitch to let him know what was going on with the chief and the photos. She also wanted an update on what he'd been doing to investigate Paul's activities.

He answered on the third ring. "Mitchell."

"It's Margot."

He laughed. "You do know I have caller ID, right?"

"Good grief, I'm getting it from all sides now."

Mitch laughed again. "Getting what?"

"Sarcasm. Cops and private investigators. You're all full of it. Why is that?"

"It's a defense mechanism. We see so much ugliness and evil that we use humor and snide remarks as a coping tool. It's almost an epidemic in police forces around the world."

"I'm worn out from it. Can we call a small truce and stop for a while?"

"I'm game. Not so sure about your cop friend but I'm in."

"Good. Now that we have that out of the way, what's the latest news on Paul and his wife?"

"Not much. I went out to the place where he works but didn't speak to anyone since there was only one other person on duty and I was afraid they were pals. You know, a forestry service worker in a rural area is hard to do surveillance on."

"I can only imagine."

She'd known, when Mitch initially found Murdock by hacking into a federal database, that getting any real information on him and his daily activities would be hard. She really only wanted to stop him from killing again as well as make him pay for what he'd already done but she also knew she needed good data on his schedule and movements to be successful in her quest.

"When he's draws the duty—which he did this week by the way—to sit in the tower and watch for fires north of the city, there's really no way to spy on him since there's nothing out there but trees and some workers cutting down the pines for the paper mill."

"Couldn't you be a camper in one of the National Forests?" She cranked the engine and pulled out of the police station parking lot onto the street.

"I sense a bit of sarcasm there, Margot."

"From me? Never." She giggled then turned serious. "Do you think we have a chance in hell in succeeding?"

"I sure hope so. I don't want to see another woman die at the hands of Paul Murdock. He's a menace and has to be stopped. Did you have any luck at the police station with your detective?"

"It's moving along there. The chief has gotten on board in a big way so I'm hopeful for action soon. He was pretty hot when he saw what we found. I could tell then that he didn't like sloppy police work and, in his mind, someone in both Reno and New Orleans each dropped the ball."

"Good. Maybe they'll start a task force or something."

"A task force seems extreme for one guy."

"Happens all the time with a suspected serial killer."

"Isn't that usually before they find out who it is?" She continued down the road toward the bridge leading to Gulf Breeze to return to the beach to relax a while before the planned drink with Richard.

"Since this is a three city investigation now, they'll have to put some key people together to work out the multi-jurisdictional issues. I imagine both the other cities will send someone post haste."

"So that's a *good* thing? Seems to me that it wouldn't be since we'll be more likely to be left out of the loop, right?"

"All the more reason to be friendly with Detective

Richard Higgins. You should make yourself someone he wants to trust and confide in."

"That sounds kind of underhanded."

"It is what it is, lady. Do you want to win or not?"

"You know I want to win. I *have* to."

"There ya go then. Sometimes underhanded is the only way to go."

She shook her head. Sadly, no matter how much she wanted him to be wrong, Mitch was right. She had to do what she had to do. For Geneva. Margot wiped away a tear. And for Jill and Patricia.

CHAPTER 7

"Let no guilty man escape, if it can be avoided. No personal consideration should stand in the way of performing a public duty." *Ulysses S. Grant, Eighteenth President of the United States (1822-1885)*

Wearing the prettiest dress she packed—the dark pink one with the spaghetti straps and small flowers—the one that was way out of her comfort zone, Margot drove toward the bar where she agreed to meet Richard. As she moved along, she tugged at the little shoulder sweater her friend had convinced her to buy as a cover up for cold restaurants and bars. Why was she dressing as if she were on a first date and trying to impress a man? This was business.

It had been a long time since she'd met *any* man for an evening out and she was as skittish as a cat, even though she knew there wasn't any need to be.

Some jackass in an aggressive truck whipped past her on the bridge into Pensacola. He honked a long time as he sailed by. She shrugged her shoulders. She was going the speed limit and if that idiot had an issue with it, too bad for him.

Once she came into the city, she made her way to the parking lot across the street from Seville Quarter, a complex of several bars on Government Street.

Margot parked and walked past the antique fire engine sitting outside the door. She asked the bouncer at the door how to get to the End of the Alley Bar and giggled a little when he pointed down the corridor and said, "At the end of the alley."

Passing by three other bars as well as the restrooms, Margot strolled down a hallway paved with old bricks. Her spiky heels got caught a couple of times in the grout. Hoping not to sprain her ankle before she could reach a glass of wine, she stumble-walked to the door ahead of her at the end of the corridor. Once there, she opened it and was surprised to see the open sky over her head.

To her delight, the outdoor bar was an oasis in the city. There were plants all around. Ferns and tall trees were placed around the perimeter as well as circling a fountain off to one side of the area where a bartender was at work. The chairs arrayed at the tables were tall rattan with fan-backs. It almost was as if she'd been transported to some Pacific island. Delighted at the atmosphere, Margot addressed the woman seating guests. "I'm meeting a friend. He's handsome, has dark, somewhat curly, hair and has a smile that—"

"Lights up the city?" the woman asked.

"How'd you know?"

"He's sitting right over there." She nodded in the general direction of the right back corner of the building.

"So you think he's cute, too?" Margot couldn't believe she was asking a stranger such a question. What was wrong with her and what happened to the woman who kept everything under tight lock and key and never let it out?

"Not really. I went to high school with him and remember him as a scrawny kid who didn't have his growth spurt until college."

"He sure filled out nicely once he decided to, you have to admit." Margot wanted to slap her hand over her mouth. Geez. Something really was wrong with her. This woman admitted she was friends with Richard and now Margot was giving her information that wouldn't be good if the lady told Richard. No way did Margot want him to know she thought he was attractive. Oh what use of that he might make in one of his sarcastic moments.

"I guess I would grudgingly admit to it." The hostess laughed. "Come on, I'll take you to him. Watch out, though. He's been a heartbreaker since his marriage ended. Don't get too attached."

Curious about that statement but already halfway to

the table where Richard sat looking devastatingly handsome in a white open collar shirt and a navy blazer, Margot decided to save her questions for when she could sneak out to the ladies' room. When she *did* get a chance to chat with the woman, she hoped to be able to ferret out some of Richard's secrets.

Richard stood as they approached the table. "Hello again, Gina." He nodded at the hostess then turned to Margot and indicated the other chair. "Miss Jenkins."

Margot took the indicated seat. "Surely we're not back to calling each other by our surnames, are we?"

"Your waitress will be by in a moment." Gina said before she returned to her podium.

"High school, huh?"

Richard's face registered shock. "She told you that?"

"Yeah."

"You've known her about five seconds and she told you we went to high school together? How does that even come up in that time frame?"

"Beats me." Margot truly hoped he never found out exactly how it *did* arise.

"Never mind." He ran his hand across the tabletop. "You wanted this meeting. What did you need to discuss?"

"Back at the station, I made a decision while you were out with the chief—"

"What'll it be?" the waitress asked.

Richard nodded at Margot. "What's your pleasure? I'll

have another of these." He waggled his beer bottle at the waitress.

"I'll take a lemon drop."

Once the waitress left, Richard asked, "Where were we?"

"When I told you I was the next of kin for Geneva, you acted put out that I would be the one you needed to get permission from in order to exhume her body and—"

"I'm sorry about that. It was rude and I really should've kept that comment to myself."

"No, really, it's all right because it made me think things over and I realized I've been being unreasonable. I also came to the conclusion that I needed to share some information about my sister and me."

"What kind of information?" Richard tilted the beer bottle to his lips, took a sip then clinked the empty bottle on the glass tabletop.

"You know, when I decided to open up to you, it didn't seem like it would be as clinical a conversation as it's turning out to be. Maybe I should let it go. Let's have our drink and then leave. This was a stupid idea."

The waitress arrived and placed their drinks on the table. She left with Richard's empty bottle.

Richard lifted his new beer and clanked the side of Margot's glass. "Come on. Enjoy. We've been working every moment we've been together. Let's relax a little tonight. Tomorrow is soon enough to pick it up and continue. Pretend we met five minutes ago and let's chat as if we were two strangers in a bar. Which is what we are, really, if you think about it." He took a swig of his drink.

Margot sipped hers and perused him over the sugared rim of the glass. He was right. They really *were* strangers. At least they hadn't been at each other's throats since she got here tonight. She wasn't sure why he was being so amenable but decided she didn't have anything to lose by relaxing and enjoying the moment. Something she hadn't done in years. "Okay. I'm game. Let's say we're strangers. What would be the first thing you'd say to me if we'd met here initially?"

"I would first come over and ask if you'd allow me to buy you a drink and as you already have one in front of you, clearly you said yes." He grinned and nodded at her glass.

"Okay, so let's say you were Mr. Suave when you offered to pay for the drink and scored some points. Then what?"

"Once the drinks were delivered, I would compliment you on the dress you have on—by the way, I do like it—it's unexpected and delightful."

"What does that mean?"

Richard took another swig of beer. "It means it's a nice dress but it's not something I would have predicted you'd even have in your wardrobe, much less wear since it's so casual and all I've seen you in are fancy pantsuits and skirts. Besides the running gear, I should add."

"It's a dress a friend talked me into. I was a bit afraid

to actually wear it since as you say, it's out of my comfort zone, but I went ahead and took a chance on it."

"It's good to see you more relaxed."

"Thank you. By the way, you said a few moments ago that you would have waited for the drinks to be delivered before you would compliment me on the dress. Would you have remained silent until the drinks came?" She couldn't help but laugh at the look on his face. He seemed caught off guard by the question but she should have known he would recover well.

"Oh, no. There wouldn't have been silence at the table for you would have been telling me your name and what you were doing in town and I would've scarcely have been able to get a word in until the waitress came."

"You think you're so clever, don't you?" she asked with a smile in her voice.

"I *am* clever, I assure you. You'll see."

"I've already seen glimpses of it, like when you told me where I'm from."

"I'm going to help you nail Paul Murdock and then you'll be singing my praises all the way back to your home." Richard scraped his chair on the tile floor as he struggled out of the flimsy seat. He held his hand out. "Would you care to dance?"

"Do you think that's wise?"

"I don't have a clue since I have no idea if you're one of those women who step all over your escort's feet but I'm willing to take the risk if you are."

"I meant, should we cross the line from being partners in trying to take down Murdock to dance partners? Wouldn't that be a mistake? Muddy the waters so to speak?"

Richard sat with a thud and a scowl. "It's a *dance* for Pete's sake, woman, not a marriage proposal."

Now she'd offended him. It was going so well and she had to say something stupid. Had she blown the whole thing? Reaching over to touch his hand lightly, Margot smiled gently. "Sorry. I'm an idiot. Of course, I'll dance with you. Come on."

"If you're sure. I don't want to cause an issue in our working relationship."

"It won't. We can't let ourselves get off task. But this is supposed to be a fun interlude before we get to work again. Come on." This time Margot stood and offered her palm.

Richard took her hand—his was very warm—and led her over to the dance floor. It wasn't a very big area and there were only a few people dancing. He pulled her into his arms and spun her around. She was surprised at how well they seemed to fit together. She also realized his muscles that she'd admired from across the room on a number of occasions were absolutely as divine as she'd imagined. His tight abdominals pressed against her stomach, causing her knees to shake.

Good Lord, how was she going to keep dancing and not swoon? Her gut must have been trying to protect her earlier when she tried to refuse the dance. This was torture. Exquisite, but torture nonetheless.

"What are you thinking so hard about?" Richard peered down into her face.

"Nothing. Trying to keep up with the music. I'm thinking of nothing." She knew her words were rushed but she couldn't control them. It was impossible to slow her tongue down.

"I somehow doubt you have zero thoughts in your head. Based on your personality, you're never empty-headed. I bet you have all kinds of things going on in there."

"Nope. Nothing. Like I said, I'm focusing on dancing. I don't want to step on your feet."

"Ah, come on. It's not like we're doing a tango or something. It's a slow dance shuffle. What real harm could you cause?"

"Must you always talk?"

"I guess not." He sounded a bit offended but Margot couldn't take back the words. She wanted him to hold her but she didn't think she could converse while he had his hands on her waist. Good grief, what had she gotten herself into?

Another song came on. Richard took a step away from Margot. "Do you want to sit or do you want to dance some more in silence?"

"Let's stay up here."

"Can I at least hum the tune?"

Margot shook her head. "Knock yourself out."

As he hummed, Margot glanced around the space to check out how crowded the floor had become and if they still had their table. She always worried about losing her table in a bar as she didn't like to stand all evening. She actually liked clubbing better with a group of people so someone was always at the table and could watch the drinks and purses.

Her eyes scanned the room. Her heart plummeted to her knees. She caught a glimpse of Patricia Murdock followed by her husband, Paul. Scared and knowing she needed to hide her face before Paul saw her as he looked at the dancers on the floor, Margot ducked her head into the space between Richard's chin and neck.

"What's wrong?" Richard tried to lift her chin with his index finger so they would make eye contact.

"It's Murdock. He's on the side of the dance floor. He can't see me."

"Okay. I'll lead us off the floor in the opposite direction. Where is he?"

"Over to the left."

"Right. I'll take us to the other side and you can run to the ladies' room while I retrieve our stuff from the table. I think it's best we leave. This place has seven bars but none will be safe if he's moving around the complex."

"Let's go then."

Richard led them off the dance floor and over to the door. As soon as they were in the paneled hall, Margot dashed off to the ladies' room to wait for Richard to return. She really wanted to dart completely out of the place and to her car but she decided she needed to wait for her purse. Keys and her license would be needed.

Margot paced around the outer area of the restroom where the mirrors were being hogged by women refreshing their makeup. One of them turned to Margot. "Did you want to get over here to put on more lipstick? Yours is gone."

"I'm fine, thanks. I'm waiting for my friend to grab my purse since there's a guy in the bar I don't want to see."

"Oh hon, I've been there. Want me to take a peek and see if your friend has your purse or will she bring it to you here?"

"It's a he. A male friend."

"Ahh, so he won't be coming in here. I'll go peek." The woman walked out.

Margot waited a few moments and had almost decided to go on out but the door opened and in walked Patricia Murdock. As soon as she saw Margot, Patricia took a step backward. "What are you doing here?"

"I was out for a drink. Imagine meeting you here." Margot tried to be blasé about seeing Patricia face to face but she really was rattled by it.

"You ran out of my house and I haven't heard from you since. What happened? Where did you go and how did you get back to your car?"

After the findings of the morning, Margot was afraid for Patricia and had a short mental debate with herself on whether to warn the woman about Paul's history. Her decision made, Margot pulled on Patricia's upper arm. "Come over here and I'll explain." She dragged the realtor to the corner where no one stood and whispered, "It's about your husband."

"What the hell would you know about my husband?"

"Give me a minute and I'll tell you."

Patricia tugged her arm away from Margot. "Leave me alone. I think you're crazy. You need help."

"Please take a moment and listen to me. Please."

"No, I won't, and if you come near me again, I'm going to call the police. Do you have some kind of fixation on me or my family? Why would you hire me to find you a house and then disappear? And now you show up here? You must be stalking me." Patricia jerked loose completely and headed toward the exit.

The ladies' room door flew open. The woman who'd gone out to find Richard for Margot entered. The door slammed against the jamb as she said, "Your man's out there, hon and even with the ladies handbag he's rocking, he's one hot papa. He's pacing around like a caged animal. Wouldn't mind taking that hunk of meat home with me."

"Patricia," Margo said. "Listen to me."

"No. I'm going back to my husband. You better leave me alone." Patricia flounced out.

"She's not happy with you, is she?" the woman who wanted to take Richard home asked.

"I'm afraid not. I have some bad news to share with her but she doesn't want to hear it."

"That's always the way, ain't it?" The woman returned to eyeballing her makeup in the mirror.

Margot waited a few seconds to give Patricia a chance to return to the bar before she met Richard. She really wanted to pursue Paul's wife and make her listen but at this point, that would probably be stupid on more than one level.

Finally figuring it was safe to leave the ladies' room, Margot stepped in to the hall. Richard had his back to her so she took the moment to watch him. He was near the door to the End of the Alley Bar and appeared to be trying to look in.

She strolled up behind him and placed her hand on his shoulder.

He didn't seem fazed. It was almost as if he knew she was there.

Without turning around, he asked, "What did you say to Patricia Murdock in there?"

"How do you know I said anything?"

"Steam was escaping her ears when she bolted out of there and returned to the bar at almost a trot. I wouldn't be surprised if she wasn't giving her husband an earful right about now. In fact, I'm standing here to see if I can tell what they'll do next."

"Are you crazy? We need to get out of here before we're seen. Come on." Margot tried to pull Richard away.

"You mean *you* need to get away. Paul Murdock doesn't know me."

"Really? You want me to leave and you're going to stay? What about Patricia? Even if Paul doesn't know you, she does. Remember, you went in her kitchen."

He *did* turn to look her in the eye then. "Think about it. This would be the perfect time for me to do a bit of surveillance. All I have to do is drink a beer or two and watch."

"What if Patricia sees you?"

"She won't. I know how to keep a low profile. Besides, she has no idea that I know you or have any connection to you."

"It's still a big risk."

"Look, I can handle a mere bit of surveillance. I keep my face down, won't engage in eye contact, and I'll just blend into the crowd. I'm not dressed in a flashy way so I can merge with the other partiers pretty easily."

Margot snorted. The man was impossible. Better try another tack. "What about our conversation?"

"What conversation?"

"I asked you to come meet me so I could tell you some things so we could be on better terms as we try to work on this together. I wanted to explain some stuff." She took her purse from his hand. "But if you'd rather hang out here and let me head to my hotel, I can do that, too."

Richard took her arm and walked her to the opposite end of the corridor. "I understand what you're saying but I think we're already on better terms than we were even earlier today. I hope whatever you want to share with me will keep. This seems to me to be a bit of serendipity to run into him here. I want this chance to observe him. Can you understand that? Part of my process is to study not only what people say but how they act. Right now, this man has no idea that anyone is on to him—at least I hope not—depending on what you said in there." Richard tilted his head toward the ladies' room. "This is the ideal time to see how he acts naturally. Next time I interact with him may be at his arrest or interrogation which would make him way more guarded."

"I get what you're saying. I do, but I really wanted—"

"I don't want to spoil our tentative truce, Margot, but I *need* to do this. You should go so you won't be seen and I'll return to the bar. I'll call you tomorrow. Better yet, I'll join you on the beach for your morning run and tell you all I see tonight. Okay?"

"Fine. I run at six-thirty." She pivoted on her heel and called over her shoulder, "Don't be late."

"I won't."

Margot opened the door to the street then glanced back.

Richard strolled toward the End of the Alley and as he passed the ladies' room, the woman who thought he was hot stepped into the center of the hall and took hold of his arm.

"Hey sweetie, want to dance?" Margot heard the woman ask.

"Absolutely."

Margot was shocked at how much his answer hurt. She wanted to cry. How had she let herself even hope the man might be attracted to her? *And* had he really wanted to stay in order to watch Paul or did he want to dance with that girl from the ladies' room?

Determined to not let it bother her if he danced with some other woman—holding her in his embrace—Margot hurried to her car and locked herself inside before she burst into tears.

CHAPTER 8

"He who learns but does not think, is lost! He who thinks but does not learn is in great danger." ~ Confucius, Chinese teacher and philosopher (551-489 BC)

When Margot left, Richard took advantage of the woman who asked him to dance in order to get to the dance floor and try to get close to the Murdocks who were already swaying together in time to the music. As he put his arms around the stranger, Richard couldn't help but wish he were holding Margot Jenkins instead. Shaking off the memory of how Margot's body against his seemed perfect, he spoke to the woman he held instead. "What's your name?"

"Lorena."

"That's a nice name."

"Thanks. Can I ask you a question?"

"Sure."

"Why'd you send your date out of here alone? Did you break up with her because she's nuts?"

"*What*?" Richard asked, incredulous.

Yes, he may have bandied about the term crazy as it related to Margot but he didn't like it when someone else did. Someone who didn't really know her.

"You have to admit, the lady is a bit off kilter. She was all over this woman in the ladies' room. She wanted to tell her something about her husband." Lenora bent her head in the direction of where Paul and Patricia were dancing. "Over there. That lady."

"What did my date say to her?"

"Not much because the other woman jerked away and told your date to stop stalking her or she would call the police."

Secretly relieved that Margot hadn't been able to tell Patricia anything to alert her or Murdock to the investigation, Richard steered his partner over to the general area where his prey was still dancing with his wife. He hoped this Lorena wouldn't keep yakking as he wanted to see if he could hear any of Murdock's conversation with his wife.

"Aren't you worried about your date getting arrested?"

"No. She can take care of herself."

"You're really not much in the way of a boyfriend, are you? It seems kind of cold you don't care if she's in jail."

"I didn't say I don't care. I merely said she could take care of herself."

They were finally next to Paul and Patricia. Richard wanted Lenora to stop talking but he didn't know how to make it happen. He was afraid as well that he was making her angry. If she stalked off the dance floor, that would be a disaster since he couldn't continue to try to overhear any of the Murdock's conversation.

Lenora and Richard sidled closer to the couple. Richard heard Paul say, "What did this person look like who grabbed you? I don't think you need to call the cops but we sure need to find out who she is."

"Why *not* call the police? She's scaring me."

"I don't like police. They get in your business and never let go. It's too intrusive to call them. Forget it."

Richard was surprised at the tone of Paul's voice. He wasn't shocked the man hated law enforcement since he was probably a double murderer but the way he snarled at his wife was kind of shocking since they'd been married such a short time. Was the honeymoon already over and, if so, how soon would *this* wife be a victim?

"Ooh, I see one of my friends over there. Let's dance that way so you can meet her," Lenora said.

Not wanting to leave where he was and not caring about Lenora's friend, Richard searched his brain for what to say to the woman.

His face must have given away his thoughts because the next thing out of her mouth was "Never mind. I don't blame the crazy lady for not putting up a fuss when you left. You might be handsome and have a body to die for but you're not very nice, are you?"

"What's that mean?" Richard was totally befuddled.

"You're not paying any attention to me. I bet that's why crazy lady left her purse in here. She was trying to ditch you since you were probably ignoring her, too. She was in such a hurry to leave, she forgot it."

"Look, I'm sorry. I didn't mean to ignore you. I like to dance but I don't like chatting while doing it."

"No worries. I'm out of here." Lenora strode off the dance floor.

Richard lifted his hands and shrugged. Left alone while dancing wasn't anything new to him since his former wife made a habit of it. In fact, she stalked off quite a lot during their marriage. He hated the moment of flashback the sight of Lenora's back caused. He sure didn't want to think about that woman he'd married.

He left the dance floor himself and made his way over to the bar. This time he ordered tonic water with two slices of lime. This was his go-to drink when he was on duty and had to pretend to be drinking. It looked enough like a mixed drink to allow him to operate as if he were a regular bar patron. With his drink in hand, Richard turned to face the room, leaning his elbows on the ledge of the bar.

Richard's eyes scanned the area. He didn't know where Paul Murdock had gone and was also a bit confused, since he'd processed what he'd heard the man say to his wife about finding out who the woman was who spoke to Patricia in the ladies' room. Richard thought Margot had given her real name to Mrs. Murdock when she asked her to show her properties. Why didn't Patricia tell Paul she knew who Margot was? That was curious.

As he took in the entire bar area, he could see Lenora standing with a few women. She clearly was trashing him to them as they were all staring daggers in his direction. He averted his gaze toward the door right at the moment Paul and his wife exited the bar.

Since the complex was made up of seven bars, Richard followed them to see where they were heading next. He ambled along the hallway. Luckily, there were several other people milling about so it wasn't obvious he was tailing them. He half-hoped the Murdocks would go home as opposed to another of the bars.

Suddenly exhausted, he wanted nothing more than to find his way to his bed and collapse. He hadn't realized exactly how draining the day had been. He knew he needed to observe the man further, and based on the conversation he'd overheard between Paul and his wife, that Patricia was maybe already in mortal danger but he was so sapped, he couldn't seem to go on.

Knowing he couldn't abandon the woman to her fate, he continued to follow them all the way out to the parking lot across the street. Only when he saw them stop beside their car and Paul pull Patricia into a heated embrace, did he realize he'd probably imagined the earlier animosity in Paul's voice. They seemed to be pretty wrapped up in each other and as the kiss seemed to go on, Richard made the decision to leave them to it and go home.

∽∽∽

Margot stopped at her car and debated for a moment where to go from there. It was still early and she wasn't quite ready to call it a night. She needed something sweet. It was one of her pitfalls. When she was upset she tended to eat. Knowing it was an issue didn't help. The craving still had to be satisfied.

As she slid into the driver's seat, Margot remembered the fast food restaurant a few blocks away. She drove north and, instead of going through the drive-thru, she went inside and ordered a caramel sundae. Seated at one of the tables, she picked up a discarded newspaper and, pulling a pen out of her purse, worked the crossword puzzle while she ate. Wanting to keep her mind occupied so she wouldn't think about Richard and the dance they'd shared, she filled in the squares on the grid.

Once the ice cream was gone, Margot headed to her car and turned out of the parking lot to the right onto Ninth Avenue. She realized as she drove down the hill that she was really close to the Aragon neighborhood. On the spur of the moment, she decided to do another drive by of the house where the Murdocks lived. It should be safe since they were still at the bar. She wanted to get another peek in the window to check out that spiral staircase. Why would he have the same type of structure built in his new house that had already claimed the lives of two wives unless he planned to make use of it again?

It hit her all of a sudden that was exactly the situation. The pictures of both dead women taken at the scenes showed that each were in almost the same position close to the bottom of the stairs when their bodies were found. The blood in her veins ran cold and she couldn't suppress a shudder at the thought of what both of these women went through in their last moments of life. Margot shook her head. Yes, her sister's death was ruled an accident but why didn't anyone connect the dots with the death in New Orleans? Shouldn't someone have noticed how alike this man's two wives' deaths were? She couldn't fathom how Paul Murdock could've gotten away with the exact murder the second time around.

Fighting back tears as she thought of her sister's final minutes, Margot turned into the subdivision and rolled past the house. Headlights behind her alerted her to someone in the neighborhood. She kept going and when she arrived at the end of the street, glanced in the rearview mirror. The vehicle behind her pulled into the driveway at the Murdock's home.

"They must have left the bar while I was having my ice cream," she said aloud. Frustrated and not knowing what to do since Patricia might recognize her car if she drove by again on her way out of the subdivision, Margot parked near one of the houses at the end of the street and turned her lights off.

She studied the black car at the Murdock's house and watched through the rear mirror as both the driver and the passenger exited the automobile. The man in the suit came around to the woman in the dress and grabbed her by the back of the neck. Margot strained to see what else was going on but had a difficult time since she was so far away.

It appeared as if the man was strangling the woman. Terrified, Margot adjusted the interior light in her car so it wouldn't come on when she opened the door. Being extra careful not to make noise as she exited the car, she sidled out. She thought about removing her shoes to keep from making noise but decided to walk on tiptoe instead. Margo barely pushed the door shut then crept down the street, wishing there were more trees in the area so she could hide in the shadows.

The two people walking to the door of the Murdock's house were talking loudly but not loud enough for Margot to determine what they were saying. Grateful that they were so focused on each other that they appeared not to notice her, she closed the distance between them. They did seem to be angry or bickering about something. She wished she could hear them but it was useless since the wind seemed to take away whatever it was they were discussing.

The couple arrived at their porch. Paul didn't let go of the nape of Patricia's neck as he unlocked the door. Once it was open, he practically shoved his wife inside.

Torn, Margot wanted to dash forward to assist the woman but knew it was too dangerous. She tried to weigh the odds of the two women overpowering Paul but when the thought ran through her head, she realized she had no idea if Patricia would help her. Patricia already refused to listen to reason in the ladies' room at the bar. Would she listen now? Probably not. All couples argue and Margot had no idea what this particular tiff might be about. It could relate to the incident in the bathroom but it was most likely something else altogether.

The two of them entered the house. Paul peered out the door before slamming it shut.

Margot stood at the neighbor's driveway trying to decide what to do. She was out in the open and vulnerable so she moved closer to the Murdock's house in order to become less noticeable. With her back against the wall, she tried to catch her breath and settle down. She knew she was being an idiot and acting in a rash manner, but she couldn't help herself.

Fear for Patricia compelled Margot to stay. She wanted so much for this lady not to be a victim like the others. Hoping to get some information so she could call Richard or maybe Mitch to come help the woman since it seemed she was in danger, Margot straightened her spine and geared up her nerve to tiptoe around the side of the house and peer in a window. She inched her way toward the opening and, as she arrived at her destination, she could hear voices raised in anger.

Still unable to make out the actual words, Margot grabbed the head-high ledge of the window and stepped up on a river rock used in the landscaping around the flowerbeds. She risked a glance into the room. Her blood ran cold. Paul had his hands gripped around both of Patricia's upper arms. It appeared to her that he was in a rage of some sort.

Margot knelt down to catch her breath again before taking a chance on another look. She rested for a moment, wishing she had thought to bring her cell phone from the car. The voices in the house didn't stop and if anything, the intensity of the words seemed to increase.

Almost in a panic that Patricia was being murdered as she listened at the window, Margot took a chance and popped up to stare in the window again. As she made the move, the rock she stood on flipped under her foot, dislodged some other stones and hit the side of the wall.

The immediate silence in the house alerted Margot to the real possibility that the Murdocks heard the clatter her klutziness caused. She knelt, prepared to sprint if the door opened.

When a few moments passed and no one came outside, Margot almost convinced herself they hadn't heard her and she was safe. Well, as safe as she could be on someone else's lawn late in the evening. She stood, almost ready to dare to chance another look.

The side door slamming open startled her. Her heart in her throat, Margot came close to crying out in terror. Biting back the squeal that threatened to escape, she whirled around and keeping low, in a few steps, covered the bit of open space between the Murdock's house and the place next door. She hunched as she ran along the property line of the neighbor's house. She kept running, taking a turn here and there as she heard footsteps behind her. Or at least she thought they were behind her.

As the night seemed to get darker, the sound of her pursuer confused her. She couldn't tell what direction the sounds came from. Disoriented, she couldn't find her car. Startled when she found herself at a dead end street that lead to an old cemetery, she barely suppressed the urge to cry. Since she didn't have her phone and chances of finding either a place to hide or a way out to a populated area, Margot made a quick decision to make her way through the cemetery. She had a vague recollection of seeing a cemetery downtown and if this was the one she thought it was, she figured she would find someone at the other side.

Darting into the darkness, she had a moment of fear of being in the land of the dead this late but shrugged it off. It was more important to get away from the murderer pursuing her than any ghost who may be about. She stumbled along. In a moment, she crashed into a tall monument. Reeling, she grabbed her head until the world stopped spinning. She held back her cry of pain but the world tilted in a weird way and tears streamed down her face. *Crap that hurt like crazy.*

Her panting breath was a giveaway to where she was. She kept moving, trying to hold her breath, and hit a shorter marker with her abdomen. She oofed out a sound and bit her tongue to keep from crying out.

Terrified that Paul would find her, Margot moved deeper among the old tombstones. She held her hands in front of her to try to avoid hitting another of the marble statues. She felt around, finally found a tall one, and hunched behind it for a few minutes to catch her breath but when she heard a twig snap, she realized she needed not to stay still. She had to keep moving whether she could see very well or not.

There was no moon but her eyes had adjusted somewhat to the darkness so she could at least tell the shapes of the headstones from what might be a person or a small tree. Hoping she wouldn't ram into another tomb, she floundered around some more in the dark.

Wishing she'd headed to her hotel after her ice cream break, Margot wanted nothing more than to sit down and cry. She berated herself internally. What an idiot she was. There was zero chance she was going to help bring her sister's murderer to justice and, in that task, redeem herself somewhat from her guilt about the whole thing.

Tears escaped Margot's eyes. Angry at putting herself in the position she was in, she dashed them away with her fists. She moved on, still hearing someone else walking through the cemetery. She wanted to wail and cry but knew that luxury would have to wait until she was somewhere safe.

Glancing around, Margot noticed a light far in the distance. It didn't look like houses from the subdivision. It was too high in the sky. From a taller building perhaps. Determined to make her way to that light, Margot sidled through the gravestones, keeping what she thought was the subdivision where Murdock lived on her right. She could still hear someone else moving around in the gloomy shadows. She was so used to the dark now that she was pretty sure she would be able to tell if a person got near her.

After about ten minutes that seemed more like three hours, Margot stumbled out of the cemetery to see a large building that she recognized as the civic center and, on the other side of that, a tall hotel with lots of lights on. She took a deep breath. A block or so away was safety. Excited at the sight of civilization, Margot forced herself not to dart out into the clearing and give away her position.

She took a few moments to assess the situation. She wheezed out a few deep breaths but her side hurt with the effort so she made a conscious effort to slow down her breathing.

About the time she realized someone was bearing down on her, several cars passed by and stopped at the traffic light on the corner near the hotel. Margot took that chance to make a mad dash toward the safety of what had to be a group of people. Her side hurt with every step but she persevered toward what she hoped was the promise of assistance.

If Paul Murdock were following her with the aim of harming her, no way would he take that chance in front of witnesses. He'd already proven he was a person who killed in secret.

She ran on, her feet thudding across the sidewalk near the civic center and across the street to the hotel that was constructed from an old train station. One foot hurt and she limped a little in a funky loping run. She would've laughed if she wasn't in so much danger and if she didn't hurt so badly.

As she moved toward the train station, Margot didn't hear anyone pursuing her but didn't take the chance to look over her shoulder as she pumped her legs to get herself to safety. No reason to waste those precious seconds by glancing behind.

Arriving at the door to the hotel lobby, Margot flung it open and, stepping inside, almost fell, due to the slickness of the tile floor and her ruined shoes. She chanced a look at what she could see of herself and was appalled to find sticks caught in the hem of her dress and clinging to her little cover-up sweater. Dirt streaked down her legs and one shoe was missing a heel. She couldn't begin to imagine what her hair and face showed of her ordeal in the cemetery but she was positive that she would frighten small children and maybe even grown men.

She walked through the lobby that was lined in deep mahogany wood and furniture that evoked the years the train station was operational. The front desk had to be through this foyer, she was sure it had to be close. She hobbled on.

A man in a hotel uniform approached Margot as she neared the front desk. "How may I assist you, madam?"

"I need to use a phone. I've left mine in my car and need to make a call for a friend to come get me." It was all Margot could do not to sob. Relief at escaping the cemetery in one piece and not being pursued into the hotel washed over her and she almost lost her dignity. What was left of it anyway after showing up in what had to be the fanciest hotel in Pensacola looking like some sort of refugee.

"It seems we need to call the police first and maybe an ambulance to get you some medical attention." He turned toward the counter. "Come along and I'll take care of you."

"No ambulance or police. I'm fine."

"With all due respect, you really need to be checked out. Did you have an automobile accident?"

"No. I'm all right. Just the phone, please." Margot realized she couldn't take a deep breath but she concentrated on making this man believe she was all right. She sure didn't need to waste time with formalities. All she wanted to do was make a clean break and get away from her pursuer.

He walked behind the counter and passed her the receiver. "What number?"

Margot gave him Mitch's number and when the private investigator answered on the third ring, she said, "I need you to come get me. I'm at the Grand Hotel and need a ride."

"Where's your car?" Mitch sounded half asleep.

"Long story. Please come get me." She couldn't suppress the sob that escaped at the end of the word *me*.

"I'm on my way. Let me grab my hat and I'll meet you at the lobby in a few minutes."

"Pull in to the front area and I'll come out. I look like a mess and I don't need to hang out in the lobby, causing people to stare at me. I'm sure the hotel would appreciate me leaving as quickly as I came." Margo cast a glance in the direction of the man who'd helped her and cringed when she noticed him staring at her. Yep, he must think she was some kind of drunk or criminal type to be in a place this nice with smudges on her face. She was absolutely positive she had masses of dirt on herself. *Please don't let him call the police.*

After she thanked him for the use of the phone, Margot handed the receiver to the man behind the counter and turned away, afraid to watch him in case he brought out the disinfectant to spray the phone after her dirty mitts had been on it. She made her way to the entry foyer in the old train station part of the hotel to wait for Mitch to pull up. He was down the street a few blocks at one of the other hotels on Gregory Street so it wouldn't be long.

She peered out the door in the split second that a black Volvo pulled into the entrance and turned right toward the parking lot. A man was driving but it went past so quickly Margot couldn't tell if it was Paul or if the interior was a light color. Panicked again, she ran down the hall and darted into the ladies' room. She would hide there until either someone with a phone came in or Mitch decided to park and look for her. She couldn't take the risk of exposure out in the foyer. She was terrified that the Volvo driver was Paul and that he was coming for her.

Inside the ladies' room, after she caught her breath from the wheezing dash down the corridor, Margot turned to face the mirror and let out a horrified gasp.

CHAPTER 9

"The very first requirement in a hospital is that it should do the sick no harm." ~ Florence Nightingale, English social reformer (1820-1910)

Early the next morning, after a trip to the firing range for his daily practice and skipping out on the run he promised Margot, Richard reported to the stationhouse a couple of hours before his shift. He wanted to see the chief and get an update on the status of the attempts to acquire exhumation orders from the other jurisdictions to allow for the bodies to be examined again with the coroners comparing the skulls of each lady to the photo evidence. Now that they'd determined there were two victims, the medical exams could be more thorough. Some things may have been missed since each were initially reviewed as accidents. The side by side comparisons should be enlightening, or he hoped so at least.

Richard knew most death certificates were not easily amended and doctors who made findings of the cause of someone's demise didn't like their conclusions questioned, but he was hopeful this time that justice would be found for these two women.

He walked in the door of the police station with a hop in his step.

As he turned toward the chief's office, the desk sergeant called out to him. "Hey, Higgins, if you're looking for the chief, he isn't in. He took a ride over to New Orleans."

"Did he say why?"

"Something about getting a body exhumed without the consent of the next of kin."

"Wait, what?" Richard stepped over to the sergeant so they wouldn't be disturbing the other people in the area. "What about that? Did the chief say what the issue was?" A bit peeved that the boss hadn't called him before leaving for New Orleans, Richard waited impatiently for the sergeant to answer.

"All I know is that he said he had a reluctant chief over in the Big Easy and he was heading over to, and I quote, "Talk some sense into a Cajun lunatic.""

"I wish he'd have let me know. I would've gone with him."

"I imagine that wasn't the plan. Chief was here at five am ready to roll out so he could be there at the start of the business day. He said he wanted to oversee part of the process and then get back before this evening."

"That puts a kink in my day for sure. I wanted to see if we could get authorization to put a tail on a suspect in a case I'm investigating."

The desk sergeant shrugged. "That's life, isn't it?"

"You're right. I think, since I'm early for my shift, I'll head over to the Coffee Cup for some breakfast."

"Suit yourself. You guys usually do."

Shaking his head, Richard turned toward the exit and pulled his phone from his pocket. He dialed his room-mate's number.

When Philip answered, Richard said, "I'm going to breakfast, want me to come by and get you?"

"Sure. I'm ready for work and hungry. We really need to get some groceries, dude."

"I'll put it on my agenda." Richard laughed. Philip was sounding more like his old self. He hadn't seemed to have any appetite the last few days and this was a good sign. "I'll swing by in a little while. I came in early but the boss isn't here."

"I'll be out in the driveway."

Richard hung up and replaced the phone. As he opened the car door, the phone rang.

Without looking at the caller ID, thinking it was Philip calling back for some reason, Richard said, "I'm on the way, couldn't it wait the five minutes it takes me to get there?"

"Detective Higgins?"

"Y—yes, this is Richard Higgins of the PPD." Embarrassed by his blunder, Richard stuttered a little over his name.

"My name's Mike Mitchell. I'm a private investigator. I was hired by Margot Jenkins to assist her in her quest to bring Paul Murdock to justice."

"Why are you calling me? Where's Margot? I skipped our run today. Is she so mad about it that she can't call me herself?"

"No, she's not mad. I doubt she's even thought about that. She's still in the emergency room—"

"Wait. What? *Emergency* room?" Richard was shocked at the sinking feeling in his gut at the news that the woman was in the hospital. Sure, she'd annoyed him and engaged in sarcastic banter with him but when had he started to care about her? He shook his head. No. He wasn't going there. He was only concerned about a fellow human being. Nothing more.

"Yeah. As I'm sure you're aware, our Margot is a bit of a hard head and foolish with bravado on occasion."

"Tell me something I don't know. How did she get hurt and how bad is it?" Richard pulled out of the parking lot and turned left on Hayne Street. Since it was one way, he had go that way then make a series of right turns to head to his house to get Philip.

"She followed Murdock home and—"

The sinking feeling in his gut returned. "Oh Lord, don't tell me. She confronted him?"

"Nope. She followed him home and saw him grab his wife by the neck. She parked her car and tried to keep an eye on them by foot."

"She really *is* crazy, isn't she? What did he do to her?"

"Margot didn't get caught but she got chased through St. Michael's Cemetery. She's bruised and has some broken ribs. She also had to have stitches on her head. They'll be letting her go in a little while but she wanted me to call you and ask you to do a safety check on Patricia Murdock. She heard them arguing and she's concerned."

"Does Margot really think I can drive up and knock on the door and ask if the woman is all right? First of all, there are reasons I can't do that myself—" Richard thought about the day he barged into the house looking for Margot. "—secondly, what excuse would I give to even be asking the question?"

"I would think you could send an officer over to ring the bell and see if she answers."

"And if she does? What then?"

"I don't know. Pretend they're at the wrong house?"

"What if the husband answers? Do I ask 'hey, did you kill your wife last night?'"

"Margot said you were a wise ass. No need to get testy with me. I'll tell you what. I'll buy some flowers and deliver them to the house myself and scope out what's up with the Murdocks."

"Let me know what you find out. I really *am* interested."

"Like hell." The investigator hung up.

Richard threw his phone on the seat beside him. He was in his driveway and Philip waited. Right now, it was time for breakfast. Margot was banged up but all right, and he would question her later. He needed to eat first and maybe think of a plan to check on Patricia Murdock. He hoped his brilliant roommate would have a few good ideas.

ϾჂϾჂ

Finally back at her hotel, Margot took a bath the best she could while Mitch waited in the lobby. She had to be careful of the wrapping on her ribs but she wanted to get clean. At the emergency room, she didn't get a chance to bathe before they worked on her injuries. She washed her face first, going slow around the edge of her hairline. Having no recollection of how she gashed her head was making Margot insane. When she'd glanced in that mirror in the hotel restroom, her heart almost stopped at the sight of the blood pouring out of her head. No wonder that poor man at the front desk wanted to call an ambulance.

Thank goodness the man saw her run to the bathroom. He was able to lead Mitch there when the investigator got tired of waiting for her in the parking lot. Mitch convinced her it was safe to leave the building after he went outside and scoped out the parking lot for a black Volvo with the tag number of Paul's car. Finding no Volvo at all was good news and Margot allowed Mitch to take her to have her injuries seen to when he decided based on her breathing pattern that she may have punctured a lung.

Luckily, she hadn't damaged a lung but the pressure of the two broken ribs on her organs was what caused the wheezing. Her head hurt at the site of the stitches and she could almost watch the bruises forming.

Margot ached all over but she was determined to keep on working toward keeping Patricia Murdock safe. She was also peeved at Richard Higgins. His refusal to find out if Patricia was okay meant Margot would have to return to that house to satisfy herself that the woman wasn't dead. Mitch was going to take Margot to her parked car still in the Aragon neighborhood. She really wanted to get in it and drive away but she wasn't going to be able to do that and live with her conscience.

Mitch suggested buying flowers and delivering them and Margot was leaning toward that as a plan since she really didn't want to go anywhere close to that house. She would think about letting Mitch do the delivery while she waited at the Veteran's Memorial Park where Richard found her earlier in the week.

The more she mulled that over, the better it seemed as a plan of action. Margot eased herself out of the tub and stood on the mat to dry herself, patting her ribcage softly to soak up the splashes of water that landed on her taped torso despite the care she'd taken. It hurt like crazy and she wanted nothing more than to take one of the pain pills the doctor prescribed and lie on the bed for a few hours, but she didn't.

Moving to the closet, she pulled out a pair of tan trousers and a pink blouse. She moved to the drawers and removed a bra and panties. Easing the bra on, she hooked the front and finished dressing.

Since she had to throw away the shoes she'd worn the night before and they were the ones she'd packed for this outfit, she had to put on her running shoes instead since the others she had with her would be a real clash. As she put them on and tied the laces, Margot grimaced. Once for the pain and once for the wishing that she'd worn these on the graveyard trip. Of course she would've looked insane in the bar in a pretty dress and running shoes. She was beginning to believe in that old saying about having bad luck or no luck at all.

As soon as that thought passed through her mind, she regretted it. She really *was* lucky the night before. Yes, she was wounded and, yes, she would probably have a significant scar near her hairline but she was alive.

She'd survived at least one round with Paul Murdock. At least she was presuming it was him. Who else would've been chasing her through a cemetery?

The phone rang. She picked up. "Hello."

"Checking to see if you got sucked down the drain. You've been gone a long time. Are you sure you don't want to take some time and rest? I can go deliver the flowers while you take a nap."

"I'll be down in a few minutes, Mitch. I had a hard time getting my shoes on and tied. It hurts to bend that far."

"I could've helped you. You could've called me to come up."

"I got it. I'm on my way now."

Downstairs, Mitch sat on the couch waiting for Margot. When she saw him, she walked over and said, "What took so long?"

"Isn't that supposed to be my question?" He stood and, picking his fedora off the seat beside him, shoved it on his head. "Is there a solid plan or are we flying loose and free?"

"I think we take me to my car and then I drive on to the park. You take the flowers we're going to buy at the grocery store we have to go past to get to the Murdock house. Once I leave the neighborhood, you ring the doorbell and hope Patricia opens the door."

They moved out of the hotel through the automatic double doors and to the parking lot. Mitch led her to his car and unlocked the passenger door. "Saddle up, then. Let's go."

"First you ask if we're flying then you tell me to saddle up. I don't know if I'm in the old west or at an airport."

"Check it out, Margot. You're at the beach." Mitch waved his arm in the air as he ambled to his side of the car. As he slid inside, he laughed. "You know, you really should've been a lawyer or something as much as you like to come back with a sassy remark."

"Look who's talking."

"Off to the grocery store for the flowers." Mitch backed out of his parking spot and they headed toward town.

By the time they drew near the Aragon neighborhood, Margot was almost twitching in her seat. It wasn't the scent of the lilies Mitch bought which Margot was allergic to but the nerves about whether she'd be seen or pursued again. She knew Mitch wouldn't let any harm come to her while he was around but it was still stressful.

Without being aware of it, Margot jiggled her left foot until Mitch clasped her thigh with his right hand. "Stop it."

"What?"

"You're driving me over the edge with that. You've been doing it since I got back in the car with the flowers. I almost drove us in to the bay to make you stop."

"Sorry. I didn't know I was doing it. I'm nervous as a cat."

"Settle down. All you're going to do is get out of my

car and into yours and then drive away. Piece of cake."

"If you say so." Margot drummed her fingers on the armrest.

"I'll be glad when you *do* get out. Now you're beating on the door. Can you sit still for *one* more minute? We'll be at your car then."

"Sorry. Too much energy flowing through my veins."

Mitch turned into Aragon and as they rode under the archway, Margot glanced around. No one seemed to be outside. She relaxed a bit. Mitch made another turn. Her car was right ahead of them and was in the clear.

Mitch cruised past her car and when he put on the brakes, Margot opened her door. She made a quick move into her own vehicle while Mitch waited in place. She cranked the engine and forced herself to ease out of the area when all she really wanted to do was slam the accelerator to the floorboard and squeal out of there like her rear was on fire.

As she drove toward the exit and neared the park, she kept her eyes moving, constantly alert for any sign of being followed. She made it safely across Ninth Avenue and circled around to the parking spots by the Gulf Power building to watch for Mitch. Staying in the car, she turned on the radio and listened to several songs before Mitch pulled in beside her.

They each exited their vehicles and strolled down toward the Wall South. "Was she home?" Margot asked.

"Nope."

"Did Paul come to the door?"

"No. When I rang the bell, there was no answer initially but I could hear a vacuum cleaner inside so I waited for it to turn off and I rang again."

"Who answered?"

"It was a maid of some sort. She had on a Happy Housekeepers uniform."

"Did you ask her where Patricia is?"

"I *am* an investigator, you know."

"Yeah, I know but you're being awfully slow telling me what you found out. Can you pick up the pace?"

"If you'd quit asking me questions, maybe I could get it out there."

Margot stopped in her tracks, arms across her body. "Okay. Shoot."

"The housekeeper lady—her name is Darcy McWilliams—she's cleaned their house since they moved in. She's not overly fond of your Paul—"

"He's not *my* Paul."

"Whatever. Anyway, she said Paul told her this morning that Patricia got called out of town yesterday by some family emergency. He told her there was a mess in the living room where Patricia stumbled and fell when she got the bad news."

"*What?* Did you tell her you were an investigator?"

"No. I didn't. It was odd. She acted a little afraid but she wanted someone to talk to. I handed her the bouquet and she almost recoiled from it. When I asked her why she didn't want to take the flowers for the lady of the house, she reached out for them and asked me to follow her to the kitchen to get a tip, so of course, good delivery man that I am, I followed her."

"Clever."

"Of course." Mitch nodded as if pleased with himself. "As we passed by the living room, I saw a couple of broken vases on the floor and asked about them. That's when she told me about the conversation with Paul."

"Did you see any sign of blood?"

"Nope. Nothing like that but the gal had been vacuuming the carpet. She could've already cleaned the floor— not that she said she found anything gruesome and I think she would've been freaked out by blood and would've mentioned that, if she hadn't run from the place when she came upon it. Suffice it to say, I think there wasn't any blood." Mitch reached out to grab Margot's arm as she staggered a little.

"We really have to call Richard. I don't have a good feeling about this at all. When did the maid say Patricia left?"

"She said yesterday."

"I guess it depends on your definition of yesterday. Like I told you when you came and found me in the ladies room at the Grand last night, I saw her in the bar and in her own driveway after nine p.m.—to me that's not yesterday, that's last night. See the difference?"

"You don't have to sell me. I get that difference, and if

Paul was the one stalking you through the cemetery, it was way after day time hours that he would've been at the house to hear a phone call telling his wife about a family emergency."

"Looks like next on the agenda is a call to Detective Higgins. He's *got* to do something now."

"He may blow you off as we haven't determined that the lady is in danger or has been harmed."

"She's not home, she was last seen by me with her husband with his hands on her neck, and there's broken glass in their house. I think there's something to investigate."

"I'm not arguing with you, Margot. I'm pointing out what I think the cop is going to say." Mitch led her over to the Wall and they both took in some of the names as they stood before it.

"I can't stand by and let him kill another wife. I can't." Margot put her head on his shoulder and cried a little.

A woman and man walked past. The woman stopped and patted Margot on the arm. "It's hard to lose our loved ones, isn't it? Was he your grandfather?"

Margot had no idea what the woman meant. She shook her head and Mitch answered, "No ma'am. It's just the massive loss of life in the war. No one in particular. She's very sensitive."

"I'm so sorry. We come down often to look at the tributes left by survivors." The man and woman walked on.

Mitch turned Margot around to return to their cars. "Let's go try to track down Detective Higgins. We may have more luck talking to him in person than by phone."

"Yeah, I agree. I'm much better at persuasion in person. I bet he's at the station right now. It's not far from here."

"I bet you *are* better at persuading the man in person."

They strolled up the hill.

"What's that supposed to mean?"

"It means you have those big brown eyes that can draw a man in and make him crazy-headed like he's drowning. You have a way of suckering us in when you turn them on us."

"You say the sweetest things—you're full of crap, but it's sweet." Margot shook her head. No way did she have that kind of effect on men. If so, she would've been using that trick for years.

"It's the God's truth. Cross my heart." Mitch ran his right index finger over his heart in a cross motion.

She laughed and took pleasure in how the sound carried across the parking lot. A small bright spot in a couple of tough days.

CHAPTER 10

"From the body of one guilty deed a thousand ghostly fears and haunting thoughts proceed." ~ *William Wordsworth, English poet (1770-1850)*

When they arrived at the station, a car Margot recognized as Richard's was pulling into a parking place near the front of the building. Since she'd mistaken it earlier, she'd memorized the make and model so as not to be caught off guard again. Mitch parked a couple of rows away and they exited the car at the same time Richard went around to the back of his car and opened the trunk.

Margot was surprised to see him pull out a wheelchair. A small one with no arms on it. Puzzled, she stopped in her tracks and watched for what he would do next. The passenger side door opened. Richard rolled the chair to the side of the car and, in a moment, a handsome, blond man swung into the chair and, using his hands, wheeled himself toward the entrance of the building.

Curious who the man might be, before the men could get too far ahead of them, Margot called out, "Detective Higgins."

Richard made some comment to the man in the wheelchair and turned to face Margot. His face went white as soon as he laid eyes on her. She'd forgotten how terrible she looked once she got away from a mirror. His reaction startled her a bit.

"This must be your investigator friend?" Richard asked as he moved toward them.

"Sure is. It's Michael Mitchell but he goes by Mitch."

Mitch held his hand out for Richard to shake.

Richard studied Margot. "You took a whipping, didn't you? I could say I told you to stay away from that man but you never listen anyway, do you?"

"I do listen on occasion but—"

"But only when it suits you, I know. I got that." Richard gestured to the building. "Come on in. I need to take your statement about what happened last night. Even though you're not a homicide statistic—by the grace of God, I might add—you *are* still a victim in a case I seem to be investigating."

They caught up to the man in the wheelchair at the door. Mitch reached for the handle but before he could open the door, Richard said, "This is my roommate, Philip Segars."

Philip smiled at them. "Nice to see you."

Mitch stepped back and allowed Philip to pull on the door handle as he introduced himself and Margot.

As soon as they were inside, Philip addressed Margot. "I hope your wound heals with no scarring. Your face sure looks painful."

"Thanks for the good wishes. I confess I have a bit of a headache. I blame on the forehead injury. The real thing that bugs me is I have no idea how it happened."

"Sounds kind of like me. One minute I was standing at a crime scene and the next I was on the ground with a bullet in me and couldn't move my legs. It's funny how life can knock us flat when we least expect it. I never saw it coming."

"I'm sorry that happened to you. I'm blessed that mine was much less serious than yours. I hope you continue to get better."

"Thanks. I'm probably as well as I'm going to get but at least the chief saved me a job. I'm now the information officer and spokesperson for the department. It wasn't my dream when I went to the academy but I get the chance to stay around my pals and make a bit of a difference here so I took the job." He smiled. "It was nice to meet you but I better be getting to my desk."

"Nice to meet you, too. I hope to see you again."

After Philip rolled away, Margot glanced at Richard.

Stunned at the look on his face—an unfathomable expression—she asked, "What?"

"Nothing." Richard shook his head and seemed to get control of himself with effort. "Come to the conference room so I can take your statement."

"I've got to get some coffee. Where can I grab a cup before we chat?" Mitch asked.

"There should be some in the conference room. There has been every time I've been in there," Margot said.

"That's because I ordered the desk sergeant to make sure it was available on those occasions." He turned to address Mitch. "You can head to the officers' lounge right past the sergeant's desk as soon as we grab you some passes. There'll be some in there. It may not be fresh but it'll be there." Richard stopped at the visitor's desk and grabbed a couple of clip-on ID tags. He handed one to each of them and pointed to the room behind the sergeant. "Coffee there."

"Thanks man. I'll find my way to the conference room in a few minutes."

Richard's face as he led the way to the conference room alarmed Margot. He clenched his jaw so tightly it seemed as if he were grinding his teeth. Worried that he was mad at her for her foolishness at Paul's house, she sure hoped Mitch wouldn't leave her alone with the detective for long. No matter what Higgins said, she knew what she'd done was dumb and dangerous and she sure didn't need him to point it out to her.

Ready for whatever lay ahead, Margot preceded him into the room. Determined to face him head on and get her words out first, she whirled around as soon as she was inside.

He took a step forward at the same time she turned. She smacked right into his chest. "Ouch. Crap." Margot grabbed her head, careful not to put pressure on the area where she was stitched. "What the heck? Why does your chest hurt like that?"

Richard reached out to steady her. "Are you all right? I think you hit the butt of my gun in the shoulder holster."

The room did seem to be spinning and her knees weren't doing their job in holding up the rest of her legs. She staggered a bit.

Richard pulled out a chair. "Here. Sit. Put your head between your knees if you think you're going to faint."

"I'll be okay in a second."

He took the chair beside hers and flipped it backward. Pulling it close to hers, he straddled it and peered into her face. "Why did you do that?"

"Do what?"

"Spin around like you did. You had to know that would knock you for a loop after a head injury. You *are* a doctor, right?"

"You know I am." Tears filled her eyes. Whether from the pain in her head or from the pain in her heart at the loss of her sister, she couldn't tell. All the pains seemed to be converging at once.

Richard leaned his forehead close to hers until they were almost touching. "We're a pair, aren't we?"

"What?" the words were a bare whisper.

"You're eating yourself alive with some kind of guilt over your sister's death the same way I'm eating myself alive over Philip's injuries."

"I don't know why you think that." She knew he spoke the truth about Geneva but she didn't want to believe it was so obvious to someone else that she was a mess over her sister.

"I see it all over you exactly as I see it in my own mirror every day. You can't hide it."

"I had nothing to do with Geneva's death, and I can't fathom that you had anything to do with your roommate's injuries."

"I did. I was his partner. I didn't draw my weapon fast enough, and now my best friend in the world is confined to a wheelchair and has broken his engagement to the love of his life in an attempt to not tie her to a man with no legs. She's pining away from the loss of him and I can't seem to get past my part in it and wishing I could undo the damage to his spine and maybe even take that on myself—"

Margot placed two fingers on Richard's lips to try to make him take a breath. She was overwhelmed by the words he let spill out in those moments. No wonder he had such a stoic look on his face on the way down the hall. It must have taken all he had in him to keep from letting it all explode out. She admired his self-control. "Shh. I can't believe he would blame you for anything. He seems like a nice guy and appears to have accepted his injuries and moved on."

"He's only been out of rehab and back to work a couple of days. He still isn't willing to let Janette in his life, so I don't think he's adjusted. I don't think anything will ever be the same. For him or me."

Margot opened her mouth to say something but Mitch walked in. "Detective Higgins?"

Richard stood quickly and spun the chair around to its original place. "Yes?"

"That desk sergeant asked me to tell you the chief is on the phone for you. He wants you to take the call in his office where the department's general counsel is already on standby. He added that you need to get there quickly."

"On my way. Stay here. I'll be right back to take those statements." He turned and left the room.

Margot patted the chair beside her. "Let's hope it's not a long wait. I'm concerned about where Patricia Murdock might be and I'm also concerned about the detective on the case."

"He *does* seem a bit on edge, doesn't he?"

"That's an understatement for sure."

∽∻∽

Richard moved down the corridor, beating himself up

for what he'd done. What was he thinking to open up to that woman like he did? She wasn't his friend and, if anything, she might even go to the chief and tell him that Richard wasn't in any condition to be working this case. He let those words slip out without even thinking.

Good Lord, how had he let her get that far under his skin?

He strolled into the chief's office to find the general counsel, Karen Sutton, seated behind the desk with the phone on speaker already talking to the chief. Richard caught the end of a sentence. "…I think so. Let me ask Detective Higgins. He's here now."

"I can ask. You've got me on speaker, right?"

"I do." The lawyer pointed to the chair in front of the desk.

Richard sat and leaned toward the phone. "I'm here, boss. I would've liked to ride over with you this morning but it's a good thing I didn't."

"Why's that?"

"Miss Jenkins was chased through St. Michael's Cemetery last night and we think it was Paul Murdock. And no one has seen Patricia Murdock since last night."

"What do you mean by no one? Has she gone in to work?"

"I don't know yet. Miss Jenkins is here for me to take her statement—she ended up in the hospital with some broken ribs, abrasions, and needed stitches in her head. She tried to make contact with Mrs. Murdock but hasn't been successful. I am going to send out an officer to check on the lady.”

“You need to move on it. I want to know as soon as you do if the Murdock woman is all right. I was calling to let you know we have the New Orleans family of the prior Mrs. Murdock on board for the exhumation and we need your lady to sign a consent form to let it happen for her sister. Ms. Sutton is working on drafting a warrant to walk down to the courthouse for the duty judge to sign so we can avoid alerting Paul Murdock.”

The chief paused a moment but before Richard could say anything, he said, “Although if his current wife is missing and he *was* the one who chased his former sister-in-law in the cemetery, it seems he already knows something is up.”

“I’m afraid you’re right. I’m going back to get the form signed by Jenkins and take her statement about last night. I’ll get patrol to go by the Murdock house to check on the wife.”

“Give the executed form to Ms. Sutton before you do anything else so she can get the exhumation order in the works. We want to get the bodies to the respective morgues so we can get some answers.”

“Chief, I think we should also get a warrant together to search the Murdock house or even to put him under surveillance or a tracking device on his car,” the lawyer said.

“That may be premature. Let me take the statement

first," Richard said. "Although I'd love to track that piece of scum."

"Can't hurt to have it drafted, Detective," the lawyer said.

"You're right. Seems like a good idea to be ready."

"Go ahead while he's taking the statement and get that done as well," the chief said. "Send the warrant for the exhumation order over to the courthouse as soon as you get the release form, then work on the other warrants, Ms. Sutton."

"Will do, Chief." Ms. Sutton looked over at Richard. "Anything to add?"

"I'll call you as soon as I have a report on Patricia Murdock, Chief." Richard was already up and on his feet ready to sprint down the hall to get to work. Things suddenly seemed urgent.

Sutton said goodbye and punched the speaker button off. "Don't run off so fast, Detective. You need this first." She waved a piece of paper in the air.

"Duh." Richard smacked himself on the forehead. "Be right back."

He reached for the paper and left headed to the conference room.

When he reached the door, he entered and handed the paper to Margot. "Do you have a pen?" he asked at the same time he pulled a coffee cup with a mass of pens in it off the credenza and handed it to her.

She laughed. "I do now."

"The chief wants you to sign this document saying you consent to having your sister's remains disinterred and her body examined again. He—and the department's lawyer—thinks we can get a judge to sign off on it without alerting Murdock. The New Orleans order has been signed already and so that's moving forward."

Margot held the document in her left hand. "Wow. I never thought this day would come."

"Not that I want to rush you or anything but the lawyer is waiting for this. Can you sign it?"

"Sure. Sorry. It just seemed unreal for a minute." Margot jotted her name on the paper. "What next?"

"I take it back down the hall and then come back and talk to you and Mitch here. I'm also sending a patrol car to check on Mrs. Murdock's location."

"Things are moving forward then. I'm glad," Mitch said.

"It seems so." Richard took the document from the table. "Be right back." He spun on his heel and left the room, paper in hand.

❦

Detective Higgins soon returned and took both their statements. Almost as soon as Mitch finished telling about his trip to the Murdock house that morning, Richard's cell phone went off. He took the call and from his side of the conversation, Margot could tell it was the patrolman who'd been sent to check on Patricia. It sounded as if she hadn't been found.

After a few minutes, Richard ended the call. "She's nowhere around. We're going to have our lawyer try to get a warrant to search his house and we're going to put him under surveillance. I have a lot to do now and I would appreciate it if you'd go to your hotel and lie low."

"Why should I? I want to help."

"Margot, you're not law enforcement. We appreciate that you brought this all to our attention but you need to step aside now. It's time to let us do our job."

"I won't be pushed out."

Mitch patted Margot on the shoulder. "You hired me to help you get justice for your sister before we ever knew about Paul Murdock's murderous tendencies and now, together, we've done an excellent job laying out the facts. You have a whole police department—heck, more than one—behind you, wanting to put this man away. You've done your part and you can be proud of that. I bet your sister is looking down from heaven at what progress we've made since we undertook this and is proud as well. Now's the time to let events unfold without any more input by us. We've brought it this far. We don't want to risk any error that would help Murdock get off for any reason."

"It's too hard to let it go. I've sacrificed a lot to get to this point. I have a vested interest in the outcome." Margot put her hands on the table and ran her palms across the surface. Thoughts were crashing in on her and she needed something to ground her. Was the police department really going to shut her out of things now? After all she'd done?

"I'll keep you apprised on what's going on. We hope to be able to exhume tomorrow and I want you to be involved in the findings. You deserve to know since you found the similarities in the two injuries. I have your phone number and I promise to call you as I get information." Richard stood. "I really need to go now. Please leave your visitors passes at the desk."

Margot leapt to her feet. "Don't be dismissive of us."

"I'm not dismissing you, Margot. I *really* have to go. I *will* keep in touch, but every minute I delay is a minute I'm not helping Patricia. She needs me right now and I think you know that."

"Dear God, you're right. What am I even thinking?" Margot flopped down in her chair. "How selfish of me to focus on myself. Go on and do what you need to do. Let me know when you find her and what the verdicts are on the new autopsies." She waved her hand at him in dismissal.

Richard left.

"Are you really okay? You *do* know he's right about everything he said, don't you?" Mitch asked.

"Yeah, I'm fine. I was wrapped up in myself for a second there. I've been praying so hard for some justice for

Geneva that I was blindsided when Richard said he didn't need us any longer."

"What do you want me to do now? I can stay another day or so or I can head home. I'm still on retainer but this looks to be wrapping up nicely here—at least as far as what I need to do."

"Hang around another day. I think I'll go to the hotel and loll around on the beach for a while. Maybe we can go to dinner later. Hopefully we'll hear when the medical exams will occur. If they're tomorrow, it might be nice if you stuck around for those."

"Not much I can do there. I'm not a medical man."

"I know but I could use the company."

"You're the boss. If you want to keep paying me, I'll stay."

At his words, Margot burst into tears.

Mitch patted her arm awkwardly. "Oh, good Lord, what did I say?"

"Nothing. I'm overwrought about all this and now that you've pointed out that the only friend I have in Pensacola is someone I'm paying to be here, I guess I'm feeling a little sorry for myself."

"I'm not your friend for pay. I like you for yourself but the truth is, in this situation, you *are* paying me. You aren't alone."

"I really am. It's become very clear to me in the last week that I need to make some changes in my life. My parents are dead as well as my only sibling. I'm truly alone in the world. I didn't let myself face that for a long time. First, I was keeping busy with my medical career and once I stopped that, I wrapped myself in charity work. Since I came here, I see my life for what it is. A shallow nothingness."

"It's not shallow if you're helping people."

"It is if you go home alone." Margot slapped the table. "Come on. I think I need to take a long swim."

"Let's turn in these passes and go. I think I'm going to that used bookstore I found the other day. They have a nice selection of naval and war books."

"Let's plan to meet for dinner then. There's a place out at the beach I've been wanting to try. It's called The Grand Marlin. How about there at seven?"

"Sounds good."

They stood and walked together to the desk sergeant's area. As they signed out, Philip rolled by. He stopped. "All done?"

"We are. It was nice to meet you." Margot smiled. "I hope your day is going well."

"It is. I'm glad to be back at work. There's always something to do around here. I thought it was going to be hard to be back at the station not in uniform but I find it's still in my blood whether I can walk or not."

Wanting to have a conversation with Philip regarding his situation since Richard told her about his feelings of guilt about his roommate's injuries but not quite knowing how to broach the subject, she said, "I'm glad to hear it. I bet the other officers who work here are happy you've returned."

"I think they are. There's some who've acted a bit like they think I'm breakable but you know what?"

"What?"

"I've found that even though I *am* broken physically, I can still offer my brains to the operations here."

"That's great, man. I love that attitude since I've known some guys who *aren't* injured who have less to offer than that," Mitch said.

"Speaking of things to offer, I guess your wife or girl-friend thanks God every day that you survived." Margot knew he'd broken off with his girl since Richard said so but she wanted to see what the man would say.

"I have no girlfriend."

"I can relate. I have no one waiting at home either." Margot smiled. "Oh, wait, I forgot you have Detective Higgins. He must be fun to come home to."

Philip laughed. "Maybe I should get a dog."

"Funny you should say that. Margot and I were talking a few moments ago about how to make life more mean-ingful. She needs to get out more and it sounds like may-be you do as well. We're going to The Grand Marlin for dinner. Would you like to join us?" Mitch asked.

Philip appeared to think about it for a few moments. "I think I'd like that. I don't drive at night right now as I'm still getting used to the especially equipped van I just got—"

"I can pick you up. I'm staying in town. Margot's on the beach."

"I was going to say I'd take a cab but if you want to come by and get me, that would be great. I'm pretty close to the station here."

"Be glad to come by for you. It's going to be a nice evening. We were thinking seven so how about I come by at a quarter til?"

"Sounds good." Philip reached up and grabbed a note pad off the counter. He jotted something and handed it to Mitch. "My address and cell number."

"Great. See you tonight then." Margot reached her hand out to shake Philip's. "We can help each other get back out in the social scene. It's been too long for me, too."

Philip squeezed her hand. "It's been hard but I think starting slow and with two people I can see as friends with no complications should make it easier."

"I like that way of looking at it. No complications." Margot took her hand back and smiled. "See you in a little while."

"Looking forward to it." Philip rolled away as Margot and Mitch left the station.

CHAPTER 11

Margot wore her yellow bathing suit with the periwinkle colored flowers. It was her favorite suit and covered the tape that held her broken ribs since it was a tank with a small skirt attached. She sat in one of the deck chairs on the sand and debated whether to go in the water since it was warm. The sweat trickled down her spine. The combination of her body oils and the lycra fabric along with the tape was disgusting her. It was almost as if she were in a sauna.

When she could bear it no longer, she stood and strode to the shoreline. The bathwater temperature water lapped at her toes, tempting her even more to jump in. she spoke to herself out loud as if she needed to convince herself what she was about to do was okay. "I have more tape for my ribs and can rewrap them. I know what I'm doing."

A couple of young boys ran by in the shallow break-water. They laughed as they chased each other, reminding Margot of family trips to the beach when she and Geneva were children. Tears streamed down her cheeks as it hit home again how alone she was since her parents and Geneva died. Determined to chase those demons out of her head, Margot strode into the surf until the blue-green water was over her knees.

Once she was in that deep, she dove under the water and even though her ribs ached at the exertion, swam for as long as she could hold her breath. When she came up for air, she floated on her back in the salt water. The surf wasn't bad. A few swells here and there, which served to lull her into a calm state. She mulled over the last days and, with a feeling of pride, decided she had really done something extraordinary as Mitch and Richard had point-ed out. She convinced the police to open an investigation into someone she believed in her heart was a murderer and a danger to society.

It really *was* a big deal and maybe a huge step in the path to forgiving herself for the past. Suddenly realizing that a huge burden was lifting, Margot cried again but this time the tears were cleansing as opposed to sad. She floated with her eyes closed for a little longer, enjoying the scent of salt in the air and the cawing of the seagulls.

The sun on her face was warm and, before she knew it, she was actually drowsy.

Time to get out before she dozed off and drowned. She laughed at herself as she returned to shore and her towel.

After she dried off, with wet sand still clinging to her ankles and feet, she strolled to the hotel with her towel wrapped around her bottom. She had no idea what time it was but she wanted to go ahead and take her shower and rewrap her ribs before getting ready for dinner with Mitch and Philip.

In her room, Margot dug around in her suitcase for her emergency medical kit. She never traveled anywhere without it. Luckily, she had a good supply of medical tape. She carried that into the bathroom with her along with some clean undergarments. Carefully removing the soggy tape from her torso, Margot gasped when she saw the bruises on her body from the crashing through the tombstones the night before. They were black and streaky all over her upper and mid body.

Shuddering at how horrible she looked, Margot turned the water on full blast and stepped inside the shower. Easing the soap over the tender areas, she focused so hard on being careful, she thought she heard someone knock on the door but decided it was her imagination or maybe the maid. Surely the woman wouldn't come in if she realized the water was running and besides, the room had already been made up for the day.

After drying herself, Margot eased the medical tape around herself again. She tried to pull it tight as it needed to be in order to aid her ribs in healing but not so tight as to be uncomfortable. She debated taking one of the pain pills the doctor prescribed but passed since she wanted to have a glass of wine with her dinner.

Margot pulled on her bra and underwear and opened the bathroom door. She turned toward the closet to pull out what she intended to wear. Out of the corner of her eye, she saw some kind of movement. Her gut tightening, she spun around and gasped.

"Hello, dear sister-in-law." Paul Murdock sat in the chair by the window. He drew the back edge of a heavy knife against his right cheek as if he were shaving.

Terrified, Margot opened her mouth to scream but before a sound came out, he closed the space between them, placing his right hand over her mouth and the knife held in his left hand against her throat.

"I don't want to hurt you but I want some answers. Do you understand?"

Margot nodded.

"I'm not going to let go yet. Come with me into the bathroom." He pulled her along with him and let go of the knife long enough to grab the roll of medical tape. He placed a strip of it on her mouth and then strapped her arms behind her back with some more of the tape.

Tears sprang to her eyes. The awkward way he'd tied her arms pulled on her ribs and hurt like nothing she'd ever physically been through before. She was also torn between absolute terror and embarrassment. She was certain now that he had Patricia and that the woman might even be dead. She was also vulnerable not only because of the knife but because she had on only her bra and panties.

"I'm going to ask you some questions and uncover your mouth to get answers but if you scream or try anything funny, I'll cut your throat without a second thought. You got it?"

Margot nodded again. She knew her eyes must be about to pop out of their sockets. She was that scared. Good God, why didn't she pay more attention when she came back from the beach or when she thought she heard that noise when she was in the shower? She could've gotten some kind of weapon to defend herself. She had no doubt he would kill her when she told him whatever he wanted to know. He'd already killed twice for sure and maybe a third time. What was one more murder at this point?

At the thought of her own death, Margot started to hyperventilate. Since she was limited to breathing through her nose, she choked. The tape on her mouth was strangling her. When that realization hit, she coughed and choked even more. About the time she recognized she was going to black out, Murdock ripped the tape off her face. She gulped in air through her mouth, all thoughts of screaming leaving her. She only wanted air, blessed air.

"Good God, you always put on this show of being so smart and so smug but you're as much of a baby as your sister was."

"Did you kill her?" the words came out in a rasp as if she'd been yelling.

"Do you really think I'm going to answer that?"

"Why not? I have no doubt you're going to kill me once I answer your questions so why not let me die with the truth?"

"Why aren't you screaming? If you think I'm a killer and am going to end your life, why aren't you yelling at the top of your lungs? The people in the next room could hear you and call the police. So why not go ahead and test it?"

"Like you said, I'm smart. I know you could kill me and be out of this room before any help could arrive. You're slick and smart yourself so I have to believe you have a plan to make good on an escape if I called for help."

"You're absolutely right. I *do* have a plan. Find something to put on. As much as I've always admired your body, I have other plans for you right now." He stepped over to her and placed more tape over her mouth. "Just in case you reconsider your decision not to call for help."

He led Margot to the closet and pulled out a pair of khakis and a pink silk blouse. "We're going for a ride. Put these on."

Since she couldn't speak, Margot snorted and tilted her head toward her shoulder.

The laugh that came out of Paul Murdock's mouth chilled her to the bone. "I guess even brilliant doctors can't get dressed with their arms behind their backs, can they?" He cut the tape from her arms. "Don't try anything funny. I'm not playing with you."

Margot shook her arms to get the feeling to return to them. Her ribs already felt better. She reached for her pants first since that was where she presumed she was the most vulnerable. The comment Paul made about her body made her aware of how close she was to nudity and she didn't like it that all.

"Get a move on. We have places to go. I don't want to be here if your man-friend comes back. I plan to be far away by the time he misses you."

She pulled her shirt over her head then searched the floor for her sneakers. She needed them if she had any hope at all of outrunning him at some point.

He found the shoes first and tossed them at her. She caught one and had to kneel to get the other.

Paul gestured at the door with the knife while she sat on the bed tying her shoes. "Here's what's going to happen. We're going through the lobby and I'm going to hold onto your arm. So far, Patricia is alive. If you make one move to alert anyone or call attention to us, I'll leave you here but I'll go directly to Patricia and she'll never be seen again. Do you understand me?"

Margot knew he was telling the truth, that he would kill Patricia, but she wasn't at all sure the woman was still alive. It was a chance she was going to have to take, though, because if there was any opportunity at all to save the woman, Margot had to take it.

"I asked you if you understood what I'm saying."

Margot nodded again. She got it.

Paul reached over and tugged the tape off her mouth again. He rubbed his thumb around her lips. It hurt and she flinched. He smacked her. "Stop. I've got to get the gunk off your face before we go outside."

"I don't have make-up on and I haven't dried my hair." Margot didn't really care about any of that but she was stalling. If she was late to dinner, she knew Mitch would be on his way to look for her. He knew her well enough to know if she wasn't at least fifteen minutes early to an event, she considered herself late.

"Where we're going, you don't need any of that. Forget it. No more stalling. Let's go."

"Let me get my purse."

"You don't need that either." Paul turned to the door, knife still in hand but before Margot could even collect her thoughts to try to come up with a plan while he had his back turned, he whirled around. "On second thought, get it. If they come search for you, it's better if your handbag is gone, too."

She hadn't thought of that and now regretted even mentioning the purse. Mitch would definitely have known there was trouble if she had left the bag. "Can I ask you a question?"

Murdock reached out and grabbed hold of her arm. "No. Come on. Let's get out of here."

Trying to move slowly through the hallway to waste more time, Margot was stunned when Paul jerked her toward the elevator. "Quit it. I'll cut your throat right here if you don't stop trying to call attention to yourself."

"Okay. Okay. Don't hurt me." Tears sprang to her eyes. She knew in that moment that she was doomed. She'd never get free and she'd never find her way to the new life she wanted to make for herself. The one she had almost convinced herself she deserved since she'd gotten the police to believe her sister was murdered. She could hardly take in the fact that she would be dying at the hands of the same man.

"Then act right. Get on this elevator and behave as if you're on vacation with your boyfriend. In other words, stand close to me. If you move too far away or try to make a run for it, I'll catch you and I *will* kill you as soon as we're out of public."

"I got it."

The door to the elevator opened. There were two other people on the car. Margot took a step back but Paul pushed her forward. "Go ahead, darling. It's big enough for all of us."

She stepped on, followed by the mad man with the knife. He stood so close to her back she sensed each exhalation of breath on her neck. With great effort she forced herself not to shudder at the intimacy of his presence. She had no doubt he'd do what he said and she was afraid for the people in the elevator with them.

When the doors opened, Margot whipped around so fast to exit she almost lost her balance. Paul grabbed her upper arm close to her breast. He ran his hand along the area. She did shudder in horror then. The man was absolutely mad, and she feared now that he might rape her before he killed her. Somehow she could face her own death easier than that prospect.

They walked down the corridor to the lobby. He whispered in her ear, "You're doing well but can you smile a little? You look pale and afraid. This is not how we need to stroll out of here."

Great. Now he wanted her to look like she was having a grand time? She *was* afraid. How do you not look scared if you were? She wasn't an actress. She was a doctor. As soon as that thought passed through her numb brain, she realized it was true. By God, she *was* a doctor in her heart of hearts.

Margot straightened her spine. Maybe after all this time and after quitting her medical career over the guilt of her sister, she was ready to face the fact that she was meant to be a physician. Somehow even though she might die in the next few minutes or hours, facing this important facet of her personality gave her incredible strength and nerve. She actually smiled at the desk clerk when the woman called out a greeting to her.

"Nicely done on the smile but don't speak to her." Paul was breathing in her ear again.

"Fine." Margot didn't speak but she did acknowledge the lady by inclining her head in a greeting to go along with the smile. Paul had no idea that his command not to speak to the lady would probably alert her that something was amiss—something besides Margot not being groomed to her usual standard. Margot stopped on her way out of the hotel and spoke to this lady each time she left. They'd struck up a kind of friendship and this walking past with no greeting would—hopefully—cause concern.

They left through the automatic double doors. Paul walked/dragged Margot to his black Volvo. He clicked the key fob, unlocking the door. He opened the passenger side door and shoved her a little. She slid in and sat, thinking she could open the door and escape as he walked around to his side but she suppressed the urge as soon as Patricia's face popped up in her head. She couldn't abandon her. If Patricia was alive, Margot wanted to help her.

Paul opened his own door and got in. "I was half hoping you'd take this chance to run."

"I considered it."

"I figured the brilliant doctor would think she was so smart she could outrun a knife and I really, really wanted you to try."

"Like I said, I thought about it."

He cranked the engine. "What stopped you?"

"Your current wife."

"Ah, I see. The do-gooder wants to save the third Mrs. Murdock. How very, very noble of you."

"I don't know why I'm trusting you when you tell me she's alive and I may be risking my own safety for no reason but if there's even any hope Patricia is alive, I *have* to try to help her."

"I always thought you had delusions of grandeur. How the hell do you think you're going to help her when you're as much as prisoner as she is?" He backed out and headed to the exit.

"I don't know but I'm willing to see if I can." Margot stared out the window, watching where he was going. Surprised he didn't stay on the road that led off the beach and that he took a left at the traffic light near Flounders restaurant, she glanced over at him. Her eyes widened when she noticed the gun in his lap.

"I thought I might share with you that I have more at my disposal than a mere knife. I suggest you stay quiet when we get to the guard shack up here. I'm going to place this out of sight but not out of reach. If you make one wrong move, first I kill the guard, then you. Got it?"

"Got it." Margot faced facts. She was an idiot. Patricia was probably already dead and now she herself was out of options.

The sun was lower in the sky and Margot hoped it was getting close to dinnertime. Of course, even when Mitch missed her and tried to find her at the hotel, he wouldn't know where to go from there to actually locate and save her. She was going to have to do this herself. Once she ascertained if Patricia was still alive.

Paul pulled up to the entrance to Fort Pickens, a national seashore park at the end of Via DeLuna Drive. He chatted with the guard as if he were a tourist and even laughed at something the man said. He showed the officer his parking pass and told some story about being at the campground with his motorhome.

Realizing that others would be around a crowded campground, Margot let herself hope for a moment that she could find a way to get a message to Mitch or the police.

Mitch would be much closer to the park since he would already be on the beach at the restaurant so she made up her mind to call him first. He could ring for reinforcements.

Paul drove past the campground and her hopes were dashed. Where could he be taking her? She'd not been down this road so had no idea what else was out here.

Soon enough, Paul brought the car to a stop in front of some kind of old brick structure. "Here we are." He turned the key to the off position.

"What is this place?"

"It's called Fort Pickens. I would've thought a genius like you could read the signs."

"There's no way you have Patricia out here. Someone

would have seen her and saved her. She's really dead, isn't she?"

"Come and see." Paul tucked the pistol in the back of his waistband and pulled a light jacket from the backseat. He tugged it on and opened his door. "Let's move."

She opened her own door, debating again making a dash for it. The place was almost deserted but she noticed a family of four playing around on one of the mounds and didn't want to expose them to the danger of a gun. The thought raced through her head that she had probably missed a lot of chances to get away from this man because of her fears for others. Why wasn't she as afraid for herself? She wasn't some kind of hero. No. Not at all.

Determined to get herself out of this mess, Margot turned away from Paul and took several steps.

"Where do you think you're going?" He grabbed her arm. He must have run around the car to get to her so fast.

"I'm finished cooperating with you. It's clear now that Patricia is already dead. There's nowhere out here for you to have her imprisoned so I've decided I'm going to look out for myself."

"How admirable as well as stupid of you."

Paul slid the knife Margot hadn't noticed he was holding down her arm. The sting of the fresh cut took her breath away. Her knees buckled as the blood dripped down her to her hand.

"That's merely a taste of what's to come if you don't

do what I say and do it now." He held her up and led her toward the interior of the fort. "Keep your mouth shut and let's go."

Shocked that he actually used the knife on her where anyone could see, Margot could do nothing but follow along with him. Concerned at the rate of blood loss, she tried to calculate in her head how much time she had if he didn't allow her to bind the wound.

He led her through a maze of rooms inside the fort until they went inside a place that was almost pitch dark. "Where are we?" she asked.

"This is called a battery. The soldiers used them for storage. It's really a perfect place for what I have planned. No one really comes into the deepest areas and that's even truer in the nights. They used to be open in the evenings for the people in the campgrounds but over the years, too many people were hurt playing in the dark so they closed them after dusk and some of the deeper areas have been roped off for years. That's why I could keep that wife of mine out here today."

"Why did you suddenly decide she needed to die and how did you get her out here with no one seeing you?"

"I have friends who set me up with a campground pass and I brought her out here at three am. After that fiasco in the cemetery and my failure to grab you at the Grand, I went back to the house and forced her to tell me what was going on."

"What did she tell you?"

"About some conversation in the ladies room at the bar and a woman by the name of Jenkins trying to buy a home from her. I'm pretty bright myself and figured out it could only be the arrogant doctor sister-in-law behind any investigation of me and my tragic widowhood. After all, my first wife's maiden name was Jenkins. It was kind of stupid of you to use your real name, Margot.

"I called a friend in Reno today and learned some other interesting facts so it was then only a matter of finding out your hotel and coming to get you. Patricia was kind enough to let me know you were staying at the beach."

"How did you find my room number? I know the desk didn't give it to you." They continued to walk deeper into the darkness. Margot wasn't sure she could find her way out if she *did* get free and wasn't a little dizzy from blood loss.

"I watched you this afternoon on the beach and in the water then followed you at a discreet distance to your room. I *do* have to say, Margot dear, that even though your sister was the champion swimmer that you fill out your own suit quite nicely. It makes me wonder which sister is better in the sack."

"You're disgusting." Margot spat on the ground. "Don't you dare speak of my sister."

"I'll do and say what I want. I'm in charge here and don't you forget it." He turned the corner. "Look—if your eyes have adjusted to the dark that is—here's your friend Patricia now."

Margot, following too close on his heels, slammed into Paul's back. He stumbled a little but regained his balance before she could shove him to the ground. She peered around him to see Patricia seated on the dirty floor. Her feet and hands were tied and she had a rag in her mouth. Her eyes were round and terrified. They almost glowed in the dark they were so white and wide.

CHAPTER 12

"It does not do to leave a live dragon out of your calculations if you live near him." ~ J.R.R. Tolkien, English writer and poet (1892-1973)

When Margot didn't appear for dinner, Mitch went into overdrive. She was crazy enough to try to find Patricia when she promised she wouldn't. He didn't want to panic but he knew he had to act fast. He asked Philip to accompany him to Margot's hotel to see if she'd been delayed.

He didn't really think so because she would normally have called. She didn't answer either the cell or the room phone so he decided to head to the hotel to see what was what.

They arrived at the desk and spoke to the manager. In response to Mitch's question about the last time she'd seen Margot, the woman stated it had been less than two hours earlier.

"Was there anything odd about the encounter?" Philip asked.

"It's interesting you ask that. She was definitely not her normal friendly self."

"I see her rental car is still in the parking lot. Do you know if she walked somewhere?" Mitch knew that couldn't be true since she was supposed to meet them and while the restaurant could be considered to be within walking distance, he knew Margot well enough to know she wouldn't have made the trek. It was humid out and the walk was close to two miles. She was a runner but not in a dress and heels which she would wear to a nice dinner.

"Actually, she was with a tall blond-haired man who seemed to discourage her from talking to me. Usually she comes over to the desk and chats. The other weird thing was her hair was wet and looked as if she hadn't taken time to even brush it. She also had on zero makeup. Miss Jenkins isn't one to look prissy but she at least always wore a trace of makeup and lipstick. It was strange."

"Can you describe the man a little more? Under six feet or over? Thin or overweight?"

"Um. Let me think." The lady glanced around the lobby. "See that man over there by the coffee urn?"

Mitch turned his head to check him out. He looked back at the manager. "Yeah?"

"He was about that height and build. Very handsome as well. Almost model-like attractive."

Mitch faced Philip. "Sounds like Murdock for sure."

"I wonder how he found her." Philip addressed the manager. "Is there any camera footage of the parking lot?"

"Good idea," Mitch agreed. "Maybe we can find his car and see if she got in and which way they went from here."

"There are some cameras around the perimeter of the building but the parking lot isn't under surveillance," the manager said.

"Let me call Richard. See what he wants us to do," Philip said.

"Can I see her room? To see if anything is missing or if there was a struggle?" Mitch asked.

"Wait, don't do that yet. It may be a crime scene and since we know she left the premises, it'll be better to get a forensics unit in there." Philip held up his phone. "Dialing Richard now."

"Let's at least look at the last couple hours of tape. Maybe the blond man parked close enough to the building that we can see if his car is out there," the manager said.

"Sounds like something to do anyway. Maybe we'll get lucky," Mitch said.

"Come around the corner and I'll let you in the back where the monitors are located." The manager pointed to the left. Mitch nodded to Philip who was talking on the phone and the two men met the woman at the door to the office.

Inside the room, the manager picked up a remote control-like device and queued up the camera to five pm. "We can fast forward if you know what kind of car it is."

"Black Volvo."

Philip disconnected his call. "Richard got a warrant to put a tracking device on Murdock's car as well as permission to follow him. The man's car is in his driveway and hasn't been moved all afternoon. The patrol officers assigned to follow him haven't seen him around at all. Richard's on his way out here. He's also sending a crime scene unit to process the room."

"That's all well and good but now we have two missing women and no idea what kind of car Murdock is in." Mitch was ready to pull his hair out. This was crazy. How had they gotten here? He knew he shouldn't have let Margot out of his sight today.

"Here's a black Volvo now," the manager said.

"Fast forward to see if they come out and get in it." Mitch's heart raced while he watched the tape go quickly. Over his shoulder, he called over to Philip, "Call Richard back. I think this is Paul's wife's car. They have twin cars. Tell him to put out an alert for Florida tag BUU 805."

"You sure that's the number?" Philip asked.

"Yeah, I could shoot myself for not remembering

sooner that there are two exact cars except for the model years.”

Philip made the call. In a few moments, Mitch said, “Stop. Slow it down. I see them coming.”

The manager pushed stop and then play. The three of them watched as first Margot got in the car and then Paul walked around and got in.

Philip had disconnected the second call to Richard. “I wonder why she didn’t try to run or to escape when he was moving behind the car.”

“Knowing the lady like I think I do, I would bet she was told she would be saving Mrs. Murdock’s life if she cooperated. Margot is pretty ballsy and can hold her own with any man but she’s also a healer. She would want to help the wife.”

“She sure is brave if she walked calmly out of here with a double murderer and didn’t raise any kind of alarm to save herself,” Philip said.

The manager shuddered. “That handsome guy is a murderer?”

“Yep. Killed two wives so far and maybe going to kill the third one as well as Miss Jenkins.” Mitch certainly hoped it wasn’t true but he knew it was a distinct possibility. “She was probably protecting all of you when she strolled through the lobby as calmly as she did.”

“I hope she’s all right. I sure would like to thank her for her actions.” The manager stopped the tape. “Do you think the police will want this?”

"I'm a PPD officer, ma'am and I'm quite sure we will." Philip held out his hand for the tape. "We can make a copy and return it to you. If you don't mind, I'd like to take it right now so we're sure there's a proper chain of custody and no allegations of tampering if we have to use it in court." Philip pulled a notepad from his pocket and wrote something. "I'm dating and initialing this. Do you have a baggie I can place it in?"

"Sure. Let me get that." The manager walked to the back of the room.

Mitch turned to Philip. "Are they putting out a BOLO for Mrs. Murdock's car?"

"Yeah. Richard said he'd call it in. He should be here any second. He was running lights on."

Mitch pulled off his fedora and wiped his forehead. "I've got a bad feeling about this."

"Don't give up. We may find her soon. If the man was out here just an hour ago, he can't have gotten far."

As the word *far* left Philip's lips, Richard walked in. "You got that right. The car's been spotted at Fort Pickens."

᭡᭡᭡

"Fort Pickens? Isn't it closed at this time of night?" Philip asked.

Richard shook hands all around. "Nope. It's one of those dark nights when the forestry service runs the astronomy classes and the haunted walks through the fort."

The manager returned with the baggie. Philip thanked her, placed the tape in it, and added his signature with the date and time. "I figure you can look at this later. Right now you need to get to the fort."

"*I* need to get to the fort? How about *we*?" Richard asked. "Come on. We're wasting time."

Mitch and Richard moved to the door but both stopped as they realized Philip was still in the same spot. "What are you waiting for?" Mitch asked.

"I'm in a wheelchair. What help can I give? I'll be in the way. You can find her a lot faster without me."

"Shut up and come on. No one knows that fort and the batteries out there better than you. You actually did your Boy Scout Eagle project out there. We need your expertise." Richard took a big step in the direction of his roommate, determined to shake some sense into him. This was *not* the time for him to be having one of his pity parties. People were in danger.

"Okay. Okay but I'll stay in the car."

"We can fight about that when we get there." Richard led the way to the exit and to his car. "Get in and let me load the chair."

"I'll follow in my car," Mitch said.

They moved as quickly as they could out of the parking lot and down Via DeLuna to the fort. The man at the guard shack waved them through when Richard held his badge out the window. He also let Mitch's car through.

"What are we going to do about all the people out here for the tours and the classes? They could be at risk since we have no idea how Murdock will react," Philip asked.

"That's already handled. We're on a joint mission with the Escambia County Sheriff's Department and the US Marshal Service since this incident is on Federal property. We're technically out of our jurisdiction but they're allowing us to assist. It would be my guess that the visitors have already been evacuated to a safe place." Richard drove on and, sure enough, when they arrived at the actual fort structure, there were a number of other law enforcement vehicles as well as four ambulances on standby.

"Looks like they have it well in hand. I really *will* be in the way if I try to come along."

"Nonsense. I'm convinced you're the man we need. Like I said, you know your way around the batteries. We both know how dark it is in there and how easy to play hide and seek. Even with flashlights, the field of view is so small, Murdock could easily slip away." Richard opened his door and stepped out. He leaned in the car. "I'm getting your chair. I know you still have a service weapon even though you aren't a fan of firearms any longer. I suggest you keep it on you."

"I *do* have it with me. I don't know what you mean about not being a fan. A criminal shot me but that doesn't mean I no longer think a firearm can serve a purpose. I think that's all on you. You don't like guns anymore because you blame yourself for my injuries, but you aren't responsible."

Richard gaped at him for a second or two then shook off what the man said. "We're going to have a long conversation about what you just said once we get Margot and Patricia back."

"Deal, but for now, can we get going?"

"I thought you didn't want to go inside." Richard popped the trunk, went around to get the chair along with some flashlights. He rolled the chair around to Philip's side of the car right as Mitch arrived at the same car door.

"I've decided I do. Let's go around to the back. I have an idea where Murdock may have the women." Philip worked his way into his chair and pulled his firearm from the pocket on the side of the chair. He laid it in his lap. "Easy access."

The three men headed to the back of the fort. Richard waved at several deputies he knew as well as two marshals. They were left alone and soon made it to an entrance to the batteries.

"Stick close. It's hard to see in here, Mitch." Richard held out a flashlight. "This won't even help within a few feet."

"Let's roll. I want to get to Margot." Mitch took the light and turned it on. They went inside and after they moved fifty yards, he added, "You weren't kidding were you? Geez. I've heard the word pitch black before but never quite understood what it meant until now."

"Shh. We need to be silent now. In about fifty more yards, we're going to turn to the right and then in about a football field length, we'll turn right again. After that, in a very quick turn, we'll go left. Hang back at that point and listen closely because we should be able to hear if there's anyone in the place I'm thinking about." Philip rolled his chair along. "I'm hoping this contraption will be as quiet as your footsteps but if it seems as if I'm making too much noise, tap me on the shoulder and I'll hang back."

In dead silence not even broken by the sound of Philip's wheels, the three men crept through the darkness. They turned each time Philip waved his dim light in the air. They eventually came to a stop. They all strained to hear if there were any signs of life.

A faint murmuring wafted through the space. They moved forward as one to be able to catch the words being said.

⌘

Paul ran the already bloody knife backward across his face with the blunt side next to his skin. He smiled with what appeared, to Margot, to be a maniacal grin. "Well, ladies, much as I'd like to hang out here, I need to get back to the mainland. I'll return when you're both dead. I figure you'll dehydrate in a few days and then I'll set the scene to appear as if Patricia killed you, Doctor Jenkins, and then turned the gun on herself. There will even a lovely note in Patricia's writing, dear doctor. I had her write it before I brought her out here. Care to know what it says?"

Margot shook her head. She didn't want to hear what the poor woman was forced to write while in terror for her life.

"What's that old saying? Too bad, so sad? I'm going to tell you anyway. Patricia's note shows she's a true and loyal wife who sacrificed herself for her loving husband. She didn't want him to be falsely accused of murdering his two prior wives and so she took matters into her own hands to be sure Miss Smarty-Doctor didn't get him convicted on her theories. Poor Patricia was then filled with so much remorse after your death she couldn't stand it and killed herself."

Margot tried to say something then but the tape on her lips prevented her from talking.

"Tut tut. Settle down. You know, I have one more thing to talk to you about before I go. I want to ask you how you could live with yourself all those years being the favorite child? Didn't you have any thought at all about Geneva? Sure, she was a champion swimmer but do you know how many nights she cried herself to sleep after visiting your parents and having them rub it in to her over and over about their brilliant doctor daughter? Do you? Did you care at all about all that or were you content to live on the accolades and your sister be damned?"

Margot couldn't believe her ears. He thought *she* was the favored child, not Geneva? And who was he to act like he cared when he was the one who killed her? How much could he really have minded the way her parents treated her if he was willing to murder her?

"I was quite sorry for my lovely wife for a number of years. Of course, later, she became worth more dead than alive. I dreamed of Olympic gold medals for her with all the endorsements and other perks that would entail. She was set to win at least four and then she had to get sick and miss that season. We were already on site for the games and she had to be airlifted out of there. It was so inconsiderate of her. After that disappointment and no multi-million dollar deals, I had to do something. My creditors were chasing me." Paul laughed. "Never mind. Forget I said that. I'm not confessing to anything." He bowed. "Adieu, ladies."

Murdock turned and walked away with a cocky stroll. Margot's gut sank almost to her toes as she lost hope for escaping from this bunker. She'd been frantically working at the tape at her hands and feet but it seemed all she succeeded in doing was pulling it tighter. It was dark and getting colder by the minute. She didn't know what else to do. Every time she glanced over at Patricia, the other woman was sitting still with her eyes closed as if she'd already given up.

A loud noise in the corridor startled her. Was that a gunshot?

Patricia's head popped up. Her eyes wide, she tilted her head in the direction Paul had gone.

Margot shrugged her shoulders. As confused as Patricia at what may be happening, she didn't have a clue what all the noise was about. It did seem as if guns were going off and the sound was reverberating off the walls. Margot wondered for a moment if this was the way the fort sounded back in the days when it was used as protection from invasion.

Placing her head on her knees, Margot prayed that whomever was firing the gun was on her side and that rescue was at hand. She wasn't sure how it could happen but maybe, just maybe, Mitch and Richard found a way to find her. Could they have traced his car in the parking lot?

In a few moments, someone touched Margot on the right shoulder. She practically leapt out of her clothes but recovered herself as soon as Richard knelt beside her and scooped her into a hug. Even in the darkness, she recognized him by his scent and the strength in the arms that had held her before at the park.

"Are you all right?" Richard asked. He pulled his left arm away. He patted her torso. "Is that dried blood on your shirt? It's awfully sticky."

She mumbled through the tape on her mouth.

"Oops. Sorry." She could hear the smile in his voice as he realized his error. He nodded at the tape. "I'm going to pull it off but it's going to hurt."

She nodded and he ripped it off. She thought surely her lips were still stuck to it but in a moment she was able to make words. "He cut me. I've lost some blood and probably need some stitches."

"Let's get you out of here then."

"Where's Paul?"

"He's been escorted out of here by Mitch and my roommate, Philip. There's a task force of US Marshals and county deputies outside waiting to take him into custody. He's wounded but still alive. We have some ambulances out there for you and Mrs. Murdock. I'll lead you out of here. Can you walk?"

"I'm not sure. Like I said, I've lost some blood. I was already woozy when we came in here. Did you check on Patricia? Can she walk?"

"Let me cut your bindings and then I'll check on her." Richard pulled out a knife and slit through the tape. He crawled off to tend to Patricia.

Margot was glad the other woman was seated so close to her so she could see them both. She had a sudden urge to be among people. Sane people.

Richard returned to Margot's side as she stretched her limbs to get the circulation going again. "Patricia says she's okay other than needing to pee. I told her to walk over a few paces where we couldn't see her and go ahead and then we'll get out of here. I can carry you."

"We came a long way. I don't think you can carry me that far."

"I'll *have* to. I hear it on good authority that you missed dinner with two handsome men so I can hope you're a little bit lighter to tote since you didn't get to eat."

"Very funny, but now that you mention it, I sure could use some fried shrimp." She laughed. "After a bit of a transfusion, that is."

Richard pulled her into his arms and stood. It seemed like the right place to be. He was warm and strong and all she needed at the moment. He took a few steps and called out to Patricia, "Come with us, Mrs. Murdock. Hang on to my belt loop so we don't get separated."

Things began to turn black but Margot swore she heard a male voice that wasn't Richard say, "I'll take her from here. It'll be easier for me to roll her out."

Then she didn't hear anything else.

CHAPTER 13

"Where we live is home-home that our feet may leave, but not our hearts" ~ Oliver Wendell Holmes, Sr., American physician and poet (1809-1894)

Margot woke in a semi-dark room with just a beam of light coming from a crack in what seemed to be a door left ajar. She glanced around. Hospital room. She ran a hand across her wounded arm. Someone had dressed it and, as she moved it a little, she was sure there were stitches under there. Her ribs seemed to have been freshly wrapped as well. There was no smell of sticky residue on her body. Thank goodness. Her body let off a lot of sweat in the cave that jerk took her to and that tape was awfully damp when she last was aware of anything.

A movement in the corner startled her. "Who's there?" she called out.

"It's me. Richard." He walked forward out of the shadows and stood beside her bed with his left hip leaning against the mattress. He ran the palm of his hand across her face. "How are you feeling?"

His touch on her cheek was warm and tender. Vulnerable from the trauma she'd been through, the kindness was almost her undoing.

Here was the man who'd been bantering and teasing her since she met him and now he was serious and gentle. It was disconcerting.

"I'm all right. Where is Paul Murdock?"

Richard dropped his hand to the bed in a fist. "He's been bandaged up and is at the county jail being questioned by officers from every agency in town except the Highway Patrol."

"Really? Even the IRS and the ATF?"

Richard grinned. "Strangely enough, yes."

"For real?"

"Yep." He nodded. "The man is in all kinds of trouble. He may never climb back out into society."

"Good. I'm glad. What about Patricia? Is she okay?"

"She's here, too. Overnight observation. She wasn't hurt physically but she's pretty banged up emotionally. The man she thought was the love of her life had kidnapped her and threatened to kill her. Not only does she have to face that, she has to fall out of love with a man who, as of yesterday, she thought she'd spend her whole life with."

"That's awful. I'm glad she's not physically hurt but I agree with you on the emotional recovery. That's going to take a very long time. I hope she gets the help she needs."

"She will. She seems to have a good support system. Her parents came immediately to be with her and have already started the process to move her in with them for a while."

"That's great. I'm glad she has them." Margot ran her hand over her eyes. "Why are you here?"

Richard cocked his head. "What?"

"If there's so much activity going on with Murdock, why aren't you in the thick of it? Shouldn't you be there for the questioning?"

"I'll get my chance. I was more worried about you at the moment so I came to the hospital from Fort Pickens."

"That was nice of you. I feel all right. A little sore and stiff but I think I'll be fine." She grabbed his wrist and pulled it toward her. "What time is it?"

When she got a look at his watch, she gasped. "Three a.m.? Really?"

"Yeah. That's right."

"I'm confused. What time did I get here?"

"It was around eight-thirty. We found you and Patricia—"

"Wait." Margot held her hand up. "Sit down. It's the

middle of the night. You must be exhausted."

"I am, now that you mention it." Richard returned to the corner where he'd been seated when she wasn't aware he was in the room and dragged the chair over to the bedside. He sat.

"I want to hear what happened when you found us but can you tell me one thing first?"

"What's that?"

"Why are you here at this time of night and not home in bed?" Margot wanted him to say he was there because he couldn't bear not to be and that he was so worried about her that he couldn't leave her side but of course that was wishful thinking. Of course he wouldn't say anything like that.

"I told Mitch to get some rest. He's going to take the next shift. Neither of us wanted you to be alone when you woke."

"Oh." Disappointed but glad it didn't show in her voice, Margot said, "So what happened? How did you find us? Did you have Paul under surveillance?"

"We did but it didn't do us any good."

"Why's that?"

"He eluded our tail. He kept his car parked in front of his house. It seems he hid his wife's car in the parking lot at the Grand Hotel. When he realized he was under surveillance, he crept out the side of his house and walked up the street that runs past the cemetery he chased you through, across the civic center parking lot, and to the

Grand. He then drove *that* car to your hotel and grabbed you there."

"But how did he get in my room while I was in the shower?"

"It seems he told the maid in the hallway that he was your husband come to surprise you. She's from the Ukraine and barely speaks English. She didn't think to get any proof or identification. She slid her master key in and let him enter. If you'd had the bolt on, he couldn't have gotten inside but since you didn't, she left him there. She's been fired for doing it."

"That's not right. I'll talk to the manager when I get back."

"The maid endangered your life. I don't think they're going to rehire her."

"They need to. She's learned a valuable lesson and I'm fine."

"If you had died, your heirs could've sued the hotel for negligence or reckless endangerment so I would bet the woman isn't going to be allowed to return, no matter what you say."

"Well, I have no heirs. No family left at all so that wouldn't be an issue. I'm going to do my best to get the woman her job back." Margot reached for the cup she'd noticed sitting on the bedside table. It was empty.

"Let me get you some water." Richard stood and picked up the pitcher beside where the cup had been. "This is empty, too. I wonder why since you're the only one in here and haven't been drinking."

"Maybe they never filled it when I was brought in."

"I'll be right back." Richard walked out the door, leaving it open a bit farther than it had been.

While he was gone, Margot thought over the ordeal she'd been through. Yes, it wasn't good that the maid let Paul in the room but Margot couldn't handle it if the lady lost her job over the whole thing. She still wanted some questions answered.

She could vaguely remember Richard coming to her in the darkness but then she passed out. How long *had* she been unconscious? She lay back on the pillow and closed her eyes.

"Here's your water. I also have a nurse to take your vitals." Richard returned with both the cup and the pitcher. He rattled the ice in the pitcher as he handed her the cup with a straw. "Here. Drink."

Margot drank from the straw as if she hadn't had a drink in a year.

The nurse turned on the overhead light, took Margot's blood pressure and pulse, then checked her wristband before handing her a small cup with a couple of pills in it. "This is an antibiotic in case of infection from your wound site and a pain pill."

"I don't think I need the pain pill. I'm feeling all right without it."

"Doctor's orders."

Margot crossed her arms the best she could with the

one bandaged. "I'm a doctor myself and I don't want to take it."

The nurse looked at Richard. "Doctors are the worst patients."

"She told me the other day that her name was *Miss* Jenkins. Don't doctors usually insist on being called doctor?"

Richard was using that smile he seemed to save for when he wanted women to melt at his feet and it was working on the nurse. It was also working on Margot herself but she tried to deny it.

"Very funny, Detective Higgins."

He winked. "So we're back to our formal titles yet again, Miss Jenkins?"

"No, you're not to call me Miss Jenkins anymore. It's *Doctor* Jenkins."

He nodded then turned to the nurse. "Leave the pill, I'll make sure she takes it."

"I shouldn't but I will. If she doesn't take it, let me know because I'll have to chart it that she didn't have it." The nurse hung Margot's chart on the end of the bed and left.

"I think you should take the pain pill. You're going to be sorry if you don't. You've had a transfusion and trauma to your body. Two days in a row at that. You need to follow your doctor's orders." Richard held up the little cup. "Please. As a favor to me?"

She smiled a little. He did seem concerned about her.

She took the cup, swallowed the pill, and chased it down with water.

"By the way, what's the deal with suddenly deciding you're a doctor again?" He took the cup from her and set it on the table.

Margot tapped her fingers on the bed covers. "Funny thing about that."

"What's that?"

"After Geneva died, I quit being a doctor because I was shattered. Both personally and professionally. I'd gone to medical school as a way of proving I was smart and capable and worthy of my parents' love. It wasn't because I had some burning desire to practice medicine. That's why I chose to work in the morgue. It wasn't about patient care, it was about proving to them that I was worthwhile."

"Why wouldn't they think that any way? You were their child. Of course, they were proud of you."

"There's a funny thing about that as well. One of the things I learned from Paul Murdock in that dark place tonight—or yesterday now—was that my parents played my sister and me against each other. It seems my mother spent her life telling Geneva how wonderful I was for being her doctor daughter and telling me how marvelous Geneva was for being an Olympic level swimmer. Neither one of us was the favored child." Margot barked out a laugh. "When I think about all the time I spent—no, wasted—on fretting over who Mom loved best and trying to prove myself, it gives me chills. I should've lived my life as I saw fit, not as I perceived someone wanted me to."

"And now you've decided what?"

"That I really *did* enjoy being a doctor and I want to practice medicine again but this time I want to deal with the living, not the dead."

Richard reached over and took Margot's hand from where it lay on the bed. He brought it to his lips and kissed her knuckles. "Bravo."

☙☙

Two days later—after sifting through all the evidence and after autopsies were carried out in both Reno, Nevada, and New Orleans, Louisiana, with the coroners comparing notes, as well as the bodies by using Skype—Richard was in the courtroom when Paul Murdock was arraigned on multiple charges, including federal kidnapping and two counts of attempted murder. He was also held over on two counts of capital murder. One in Louisiana and one in Nevada.

Richard was more than a little pleased at the week's work. He was also thrilled that his roommate had found a new purpose in that black place where Margot Jenkins found her way back to medicine.

Feeling happy to be alive and that a beast of a man was in jail and would most likely remain there for the rest of his natural life, Richard called Margot at her hotel. When she answered the phone, he said, "Before you head to back to California tomorrow, Philip and I would like to take you and Mitch to dinner tonight. A celebration of sorts."

"Mitch is gone. He had another job."

"Can you still come?"

"Sure. I'd love to. Where?"

"I understand you didn't get a chance to dine at the Grand Marlin."

"Very funny."

"I'm not kidding. It's a great restaurant."

"Isn't that tempting fate?"

"Not if you talk to your Ukrainian maid who I hear you got rehired, by the way. Ask her not to let any men in your room. I'll be in the lobby at six-thirty."

"All right. I'll be there."

"Wear the yellow shoes if you can. I kind of like those." He remembered how they'd hurt her feet when she ran from Murdock's house that day but they *were* pretty sexy.

"I'll see what I can do."

"See you later then."

They disconnected the call and Richard returned to work. It was kind of a slow day since the hullabaloo was over with Murdock and, luckily, there hadn't been any murders so he pulled a cold case file to look through until time to leave to meet Philip before dinner.

Soon enough, it was time to go. Richard's heart skipped a beat as he thought about what he was going to propose to Margot that evening. Would she think he was insane? It didn't matter. He couldn't let her go back to California without saying something to her about the way she made his heart race. It was a risk. God knew he didn't open his heart up anymore after his former wife's betrayal, but he couldn't let this amazing woman walk out of his life.

Maybe the dark place at Fort Pickens awakened him from his demons, too. Maybe he could find a new start like Philip and Margot had.

He drove home and pulled in to his driveway, shocked to see Janette's car there. *Uh-oh*. What was this about? Was he going to find his roommate in a bad mood? Why would she come here? She'd been to the station yesterday and this morning to talk to Philip about Murdock's case since he was the information officer but that was about business since she worked the legal beat. Why would she come here after Philip was off duty?

Stepping out of the car, Richard locked the door and entered through the garage since the door was up. He moved inside and called out, "Philip? Janette?"

Walking farther into the house, he called out again, "Philip? Janette?"

Weirder and weirder. Why weren't they answering? Richard made his way through the kitchen, then the empty living room. He moved down the hallway toward Philip's room. He stopped at the door and placed his ear against it.

Before he could knock, he heard giggling from inside. He backpedaled away from the door. This was a very good sign. He'd get ready for his meeting—he dared not call it a date—with Margot and leave them to it. Richard grinned, happier than he'd been in a long time. His best friend seemed to be making great progress in coming back to the world. Philip's integral part in the rescue of the two women from Paul Murdock had done wonders for the man's psyche. If he was ready to make another go of it with Janette, then that would be even better.

Richard took a quick shower. When he stepped out of his bathroom to grab some boxers from his drawer, Philip stuck his head inside at the same time he knocked on the partially open door.

"Hang on, man. Let me grab some jeans."

"No worries. It's just me."

"Come on in, then."

Philip rolled in as Richard tugged on his jeans and a polo shirt.

"I guess you saw Janette's car out there."

"Yep. It'd be hard to miss." Richard put on some cologne.

"It seems my accident didn't unman me after all. It was all in my head. When I found out I was paralyzed, I panicked. I pushed Janette away because I thought I couldn't give her what she needed."

Richard grinned. "And I'm guessing you and she found out today that's not true?"

"You could say that. What I really found out the other night is that I'm not useless. You relying on me in the batteries at the fort was more than an ego boost. When you first said you needed me in there, I thought you were placating me but then I led us right to Murdock and, after Mitch and I got him to the marshals, I got back to you and the ladies in time to help carry them both out. I knew then that I could be a meaningful part of the world. I have things to offer still, even if I don't have the use of my legs."

"I'm so glad you figured that out. I missed the old Philip. You were always brilliant and had so much to give and I'm thrilled you're back." Richard ran a comb through his hair. "I'm on my way to get Margot for our dinner at the Grand Marlin. Are you almost ready?"

"I think Janette and I will stay here. We've got some more talking to do. Would you mind if I passed?"

"I wouldn't, but Margot's leaving tomorrow to go back to California. Won't you want to tell her goodbye?"

"Ask her to set aside time for the Coffee Cup in the morning before she goes. We can meet her there before work. I'll drive my van and meet you two there."

"We *can* carpool, you know."

"I'd like to drive myself tomorrow. It makes sense to carpool to work but I need the practice being in traffic with the thing. You know, man up and get back in the world." Philip laughed. A true, deep sound that Richard realized he'd missed a lot.

"It's great to see you becoming independent again." Richard picked up his keys. "Gotta run."

"Good luck tonight."

Richard left his house, wondering what Philip meant by that comment and what he meant by the meeting them at breakfast comment. Did he think Richard was going to spend the night at Margot's? He couldn't be thinking that, could he? Nah.

જજજ

Trying to decide what to wear with the yellow shoes, Margot finally picked a pair of navy pants and a floral patterned crepe blouse. She hoped Richard liked it. She wanted him to think she looked fantastic. She was also running out of clothing options.

Tracing her lips with liner, Margot concentrated on making sure her hand stayed steady. She wasn't usually one for wearing much makeup but she really wanted tonight to be special. Fearing Richard wouldn't like what she was going to tell him about California, she was focused on that as well as the task with her lips, when her cell phone on the counter went off. Startled, she jumped and the lip liner drew a mauve pink streak across her cheek. So much for that. She giggled before she slid the phone to the *on* position.

"Hello."

"What's so funny?" Richard asked.

"I'm up here doing something I never do and the phone scared me so badly I messed up."

"Was it something illegal?"

"Of course not." Margot laughed. "Haven't you learned enough about me that I'd never do something like that?"

"Um. No."

"What's that supposed to mean?"

"If you'll recall the last week or so, you might remember all the laws you broke."

"*Me?*"

Richard's laughter in Margot's ear spread warmth all through her. "How's stalking to start with?"

Margot giggled. "Never. I was following Patricia Murdock for her own good."

"Are we going to talk on the phone all night or are you going to come down so I can take you to dinner?"

"You're in the lobby?"

"I am."

"Let me wash my face and I'll be right down."

"You mean you aren't already all dolled up?"

"I was until you called and I smeared lipstick all over my face."

"I bet it looks lovely."

"You're crazy. I'm coming down."

He said something she didn't quite catch. "What did you say?"

"Nothing. Come down soon. I'm starving."

As he hung up, the thought ran through her head, did he say he was crazy about me? Surely not.

Margot hurried to the elevator deliberately putting the trip down the same hall with Paul Murdock out of her head. He was gone now, and chances were good that she'd only ever see him again in a courtroom when he went on trial for all of his misdeeds. Time to put thoughts of that man aside for the first time in years. It felt good.

As soon as she stepped off the elevator in the lobby to find Richard waiting for her dressed in a nice pair of jeans and a navy blue polo shirt, her heart gave a little leap in her chest. He was almost too handsome for words, and she wondered what he was going to say when she told him her news. Would he be happy or would he give her the look he gave her that first day in the conference room when she told him her sister was the first to die and he thought she was there to confess to the deed. A laugh escaped involuntarily.

"What's so funny?" Richard asked as he stepped forward and took hold of her elbow. He leaned in and kissed her lightly on the check. The touch of his lips on her face was almost more than Margot could bear. He'd kissed her knuckles once and that alone was enough to make her yearn for him to hold her and comfort her that night in the hospital. Now that he'd kissed her on the cheek, she wasn't sure she could keep from confessing her plans immediately.

"Nothing. I was thinking over our first meeting."

Richard led her to the automatic door. "Don't hold that against me. I was pretty harsh."

"Yeah. You were but you know what?"

"What?" they stepped outside into the heat. Richard moved away from the door and toward a close parking spot where his car sat.

"It shows you were doing your job. I waltzed in there full of myself and you really knew how to handle the snob that I was. Turns out, you're a pretty good detective."

"Thank you. I like to think so. I also recall telling you I'm related to Sherlock Holmes. I was kind of full of myself, too." He clicked the key fob, unlocked the door and opened it.

"You are related. I'm sure of it now." She giggled then glanced around. "Where's Philip? I thought maybe he was waiting in the car."

"He's otherwise indisposed, as they say." Richard laughed. It was a carefree and easy laugh. One that Margot had never heard the man use. It was almost as if a heavy burden had been lifted from his heart.

"What does that mean?" She asked as she slid into the passenger seat.

"Hang on a sec and I'll tell you." Richard held up his index finger and dashed around to his side of the car.

Once inside, instead of putting on his seatbelt and cranking the engine, he turned to face her. "Long story short. Philip and I were at the academy together. When my grandmother died and I inherited her Craftsman style house, I moved out of my parents' house and into the Craftsman. I invited Philip to move with me. After a couple of years on the force—we had become partners as well when we were hired with the PPD—anyway, he was dating this woman named Janette who worked the crime beat for the newspaper. They were in love and really great together."

"Okay. Then what happened?"

"I got married. He proposed to Janette and moved in with her before my wedding, leaving me to move my wife into my place."

"That sounds nice. I know you're divorced. What happened to your marriage? If I'm not being too nosy, that is."

"She was a liar and I found out. Her actions gutted me. So, I found myself single again—no kids, thank God. Anyway, one night on patrol Phil and I got a call out to a domestic situation. That's when there's a family dispute—"

"I know. I've seen some of those when I worked the emergency room when I was a medical resident."

Richard's face darkened and he grabbed Margot's left hand. He squeezed it tight, so tight she thought it would crumple as if it were a piece of paper but she didn't let on that he was hurting her. She had the distinct impression he'd hurt himself enough over this situation. She knew whatever was coming wasn't going to be pleasant.

"We went out to this house and announced ourselves. At first no one came out or answered the door. Philip knocked again and a woman screamed. I called for back-up and Philip banged on the door. In a split second, everything went wrong."

Shaking his head as if to clear it of the memory, Richard's fingers tightened even more on Margot's hand, if that were possible.

"Don't go on if it causes you such pain."

"No. I want to tell you. I've never told anyone."

Margot nodded her encouragement.

"The door flung open and a woman ran out. Right behind her came a man with a gun. Philip stepped back and I made a move forward. The man's gun came up into the firing position and it's kind of all a blur from there. The enraged man took aim at the woman and both Philip and I tried to take her husband down before he got to her. I was too slow with my weapon and Philip took a hit to the spine. He landed on the porch and, as he writhed in pain, the man took aim at me but I was able to get my shot in first. I hit him in the leg. He went down but still had his weapon. I was still in danger so I shot again and that time I got the husband straight in the chest."

"Oh, God. How terrible."

"It was. I not only killed another man which I knew

was a possibility when I went into law enforcement but knowing it could happen and it actually happening were two different things. I also had a wounded partner and, because I had shot and killed the woman's husband, she leapt on my back screaming and yelling and beating on me. A neighbor had to get her off me."

"What an awful ordeal."

"It was. The neighbor called law enforcement as well, but the back-up I'd radioed for got there sooner as well as an ambulance. Philip was taken to the hospital. All the local guys and gals gathered there. No one but me blamed me for Philip's condition."

"And you've kept on blaming yourself all this time, haven't you?"

Richard raised her hand to his lips and kissed it. "I *have.* I think I knew you would understand since you have a bit of the blame yourself complex too."

"I've moved past it. Since the other night, I mean. I've figured out I can only be responsible for me."

"I'm moving past it as well, that's what all this has been about. Philip isn't with us tonight because he's figured out he has something to offer the world even from that wheelchair. His part in rescuing you and Patricia showed him that. He's back with his fiancée whom he had cut out of his life when he thought he couldn't give her what she needed from him. His realization that he's a viable member of society led me to my own epiphany that I couldn't keep beating myself up over his injury. It happened. We both found our way out of it. That's all that needs to be said about it."

"Wow. That's massive and I'm glad you came to that conclusion. That's wonderful and it's great that he and his fiancée are back together."

"He wanted me to ask you to meet them—and me—at the Coffee Cup for breakfast tomorrow before you leave town."

"Can we talk about that at the restaurant?"

"Sure. No problem." Richard let go of her hand and started the car. He had a stoic look on his face. "Sorry, I should've gotten us there by now. You must be starving."

"Not really but I didn't want to lose our reservation. I really want to try this place. It seems to be a local favorite."

His countenance relaxed and a small smile played across his lips. "It is. Great food."

Relieved that he didn't seem mad any longer, Margot sat and debated how she would broach the subject she wanted to talk about.

Richard parked the car at the restaurant. They walked across the oyster shell parking lot and over to the elevator up to the restaurant which was situated over a parking garage.

Inside the restaurant, Margot took a glance around while Richard talked to the hostess. Impressed with the décor, she took in the glass walls, the lovely wood floor and the bar in the middle of the room. It was casually elegant and what she could see of the food on other diners' plates looked divine. "Wow, this is nice," Margot whispered to Richard on their way to their table by the windows overlooking the water.

"You don't have to whisper. It's not the library."

"It still seems like I need to be reverent."

"You *do* know you're crazy, right?"

"I do, but that's actually all right. I think I need a little craziness in my life about now. It's been too serious for far too long."

They arrived at their table. Richard pulled her chair out. "That sounds like a plan. *Some* craziness might be good but only a little, please."

"I wonder if they have that on the menu." She sat and took the plastic covered list the hostess handed her.

Once the waitress took their orders, Margot and Richard both spoke at the same moment.

"I want to—" she said at the same time he said, "Can I—"

They both laughed. Richard nodded, "Ladies first."

"No, go ahead. What did you want to say?"

"It might be better for you to go first."

Margot's stomach clenched in fear but she spoke anyway. "You know how I told you at the hospital that I'm ready to return to the practice of medicine?"

"Yeah. I think that's great. Have you put out feelers for a new job in California? Or are you going back to the medical examiner job?"

"I've decided not to return to California. Well, other than to pack my house and move, I mean."

"I guess that's a good thing. To get a fresh start somewhere new. I get that. Will you let me know where you'll be? I'd like to keep in touch."

"I'm getting to that." She smiled at the waitress who'd returned with a bottle of wine.

Richard tested the wine the waitress poured and found it acceptable so she filled both glasses.

Margot held her up. "A toast."

"To?"

"To new friends."

Richard clinked glasses with her. "I can get behind that."

"Remember when I said I would tell you at the restaurant if I'd meet you, Philip and his fiancée at the Coffee Cup tomorrow?"

"Yeah, I recall that conversation. After all, it *was* less than thirty minutes ago."

"Before I was released from the hospital, I roamed the hallways and found myself at the maternity ward. I stared at the babies in the nursery and saw a few mothers roaming the corridor with their infants in their rolling bassinets. It dawned on me that this was the exact opposite of what I'd been doing before. This was the beginning of life as opposed to the end. My heart knew this was where I belong at this time in my own life."

"You're going to change specialties? Isn't that a lot of work? Don't you have to get certified?"

"I *do*. I found a nurse and had her get me in contact with the head of the obstetric department. After discussions with him, he and I have agreed to a plan of action to get me certified pretty quickly. In the meantime, I'll work some shifts at the morgue."

"You're staying in Pensacola?" His voice broke at the end of the question.

"Is that an issue for you?" Praying he'd say no, Margot clenched her hands in her lap.

"Absolutely not. That leads to what I wanted to say to you."

"What's that?" She allowed herself to relax a little. He was okay with her staying. That was a good thing.

"I was reluctant to bring it up since I thought you were going back to California and I'm not really one for long distance relationships—hell, I'm not one for relationships at all—remember how my marriage turned out—but now that you're staying—"

"Relationship?" Margot's heart soared. Was he asking her to get involved with him? Could it be true?

Richard leaned forward and grasped Margot's hand. "Do you know how scared I was when I knew that jackass Murdock had you?"

"No." She shook her head, surprised at the tears that filled her eyes and blinded her for a moment. His voice was so soft and gentle, she sensed how hard it was for him to admit to being scared for her.

"I thought I would die before I could get to you. I was grateful for Mitch and Philip since they kept me from falling apart. I knew I needed to hold myself together in front of them and that helped me focus on the job not on the fact that the woman I think I lo—" He swallowed hard and forced the word past his lips. "—love was in danger."

"You barely know me. How could you think you love me?" She really didn't want to ask the question because she knew she loved him as well and was afraid he'd admit there was no way they could be in love on such short acquaintance and without even kissing each other.

"I know it sounds nuts because we'd butted heads so much and, even though you're the most stubborn woman I've ever met—"

"Me? *I'm* stubborn. Lord, man, have you met yourself?"

"I have." He smiled that devastating grin that turned her stomach to Jell-O. "That's what I was getting at. We're both so stubborn and bull-headed that we can only be meant for each other. Now, I'm not saying we need to rush into anything, but the fact that you're going to be around gives us a chance to see where this will lead."

"I guess I see your point. We're both so difficult that neither of us should be subjected to anyone else. Does that about sum it up?"

He nodded. "Exactly. You've got it."

The waitress brought their food. Island Chicken Curry for her and Pan-Seared Swordfish for him. "Gosh, that smells good," Margot said.

"It does, and speaking of smelling good, I meant to tell you earlier that your perfume smelled lovely. I was going to say it when you got off the elevator at the hotel but was afraid you'd have a smart remark."

"You should know by now that I usually do." She grinned and took a bite of her dinner.

"Not usually, Doctor Jenkins. *Always*."

"And you love it."

"I do and I think it's part of your charm." He cut into his swordfish. "Not to rush this dinner or anything but I'd sure like to hold you in my arms again like I did at the End of the Alley bar."

She shivered in delight at his words. "I'd like that as well."

"Then eat up." He nodded at her plate. "You're going to need your strength."

"Are we going dancing?"

He winked. "You could say that. I propose a different kind of dancing, though. Have you ever heard that song called *Dancing in the Sheets*?"

"Does that invitation include breakfast?"

"Sure does. At the Coffee Cup."

She laughed. "Good, because I have a few friends who I planned to meet there tomorrow. On my way *not* out of town."

Richard stood and came around the table. He held his hand out. "I can't wait one more second. I *have* to kiss you."

She pushed her chair back and put her hand in his. He assisted her to her feet. "What will the waitress think?" Margot asked.

"I can only imagine she'll think 'wow what a lucky girl, I wish I was her.'"

Margot giggled. "You're unbelievable."

"Believe it, baby." Richard pulled her to him and kissed her like she'd never been kissed before, all but holding her up as she nearly swooned.

The other patrons of the restaurant clapped and cheered. Eventually, Richard let her go and bowed to the audience.

As they returned to their meal, she thought about the evening ahead and the many more days and nights they would spend together. Margot couldn't wait for the future to get started. With a fine man by her side, a new career, and a renewed sense of purpose, life was good. Very good indeed.

THE END

About the Author

Sherry Fowler Chancellor is a practicing attorney who lives on the beautiful Gulf Coast of Florida. When she's not working on behalf of her clients, she's busy penning a new story or hanging out with her friends and family in their own little slice of paradise.

www.ingramcontent.com/pod-product-compliance
Lightning Source LLC
Chambersburg PA
CBHW072158130726
47910CB00010B/870